"So, you're the accountant from Bryer's and Ridge Accounting Firm that just opened in Monkton?"

He nodded. "The main office is at the Inner Harbor. They just opened this new branch to service the Monkton farm community."

She folded her arms in front of her. "I didn't call you; my stepmother did." She failed to admit that she was totally against hiring the accountant.

"Look. . .what's your name?" His mouth hardened into a thin line, and she found it hard not to stare at his cocoa brown, long-lashed eyes.

"My name is Emily Cooper."

He still clutched the papers, looking bewildered. "Did you want to call the office and reschedule?" He gestured toward the barn. "I see you've had a rough morning, so you might not be in the mood to talk about your finances right now."

"Just give me a second, okay?" She stepped away, noting how the cool scent of his cologne wafted around her, teasing her nose. She removed her cell phone from her pocket and hit the speed dial to call Laura. Emily left her stepmother a message, clutching the phone and speaking in a low voice so that Franklin would not hear her. "Mom, I thought we'd agreed you wouldn't hire that accountant until we talked about it some more. He's here now, and I'm not sure what to do."

CECELIA DOWDY is a world traveler who has been an avid reader for as long as she can remember. When she first read Christian fiction, she felt called to write for the genre. She loves to read, write, and bake desserts in her spare time. She also loves spending time with her husband and her toddler son. She resides with her family in Maryland. You can visit Cecelia on her Web sites: www.ceceliadowdy.com and www.ceceliadowdy.blogspot.com.

Books by Cecelia Dowdy

HEARTSONG PRESENTS
HP794—John's Quest

Don't miss out on any of our super romances. Write to us at the following address for information on our newest releases and club information.

Heartsong Presents Readers' Service
PO Box 721
Uhrichsville, OH 44683

Or visit www.heartsongpresents.com

Milk
Money

Cecelia Dowdy

Heartsong Presents

I would like to thank a lot of people for helping me with my extensive research for this novel—namely, the Higgins family. Thanks so much for allowing me to visit your small family dairy farm and for answering my numerous questions. I also appreciate your allowing me to assist with the milking of your herd.

I also want to give credit to my ACFW writing buddies: Pam Hillman, Anne Schrock, and Mary Connealy. Your advice about dairy farming proved to be very useful while I penned this novel.

I would also like to acknowledge Farm and Ranch Accountant Patti Randle, CPA, for answering my questions about farm bookkeeping practices.

A note from the Author:
I love to hear from my readers! You may correspond with me by writing:

Cecelia Dowdy
Author Relations
PO Box 721
Uhrichsville, OH 44683

ISBN 978-1-60260-255-7

MILK MONEY

Our mission is to publish and distribute inspirational products offering exceptional value and biblical encouragement to the masses.

PRINTED IN THE U.S.A.

one

Dumbfounded, the accountant gazed at a cow giving birth. He dropped his briefcase when he saw the feet of the baby sticking out of the mother's canal. A rope was looped around the legs of the young animal, and a brown-skinned woman pulled so hard that the muscles in her slender arms flexed. Her eyes squeezed shut while she grunted, reminding him of the noises people made when they bench-pressed weights. She opened her eyes. "Cascy, hold on," she cooed. When he watched the birth, his sour stomach worsened, and the bagel and cream cheese he'd managed to eat for breakfast felt like a dead weight in his belly.

Her tears mingled with the sweat rolling down her face. She continued to pull and glanced in his direction. "Oh, thank God you came. Come and help me."

A plethora of unfamiliar scents tingled his nose. He swallowed, losing his voice. What was he supposed to do?

She continued to look at him, pulling on the rope periodically. "I already left a message on your answering service that it was coming out backward." Pushing the door open, he entered the room adjoining the barn, still hoping he wouldn't throw up. She nodded toward the rope, still tugging. "With both of us pulling, maybe we'll be able to get the calf out."

"Okay." He swallowed his nausea and pulled, mimicking the way he used to grunt when bench-pressing heavy weights. He followed her example, keeping tension on the rope and pulling each time the cow had a contraction. She grunted also, and their noises continued until the calf exited the birth canal minutes later. She dropped the rope, and he rushed behind

5

her to look at the young animal. He touched the newborn, awed by the birth. She glanced at him as she cleaned gunk off the calf's nose and mouth.

Her sigh filled the space when she noticed the animal was breathing. "Aren't you going to examine the cow and calf?"

Before he could respond, a young man holding a large black plastic tote entered the pen. "This the Cooper farm?"

Confusion marred her face when she glanced at Frank. Then she focused on the new arrival. The newcomer rushed to the baby cow and began examining it. "I'm Dr. Lindsey's son. I'm taking over my daddy's practice this week since he's on vacation. He told you that, didn't he?"

She nodded, still looking confused. "I left a message on your answering service earlier."

The vet grunted. "I was down the street at the horse farm helping out with another birth, so I couldn't leave."

"Are the cow and calf okay?"

"They both look fine." He stopped his examination and looked at them. "I'm glad you had somebody helping you. You might not have gotten him out in time if you'd been pulling him on your own." He pulled a tool out of his bag. "You have antibiotic on hand for the calf, right? If not, I've got some."

The attractive woman nodded, her dark hair clinging to her sweaty neck as she promised the vet she would give the new calf the medicine. Frank watched, mesmerized by the whole process. A short time later, the newborn nursed from the mother. "Thank you, doctor," said the woman, patting the man on the shoulder.

The doctor shook his head, placing his tools back into his bag. "Don't thank me. You two got him out in time." He told Emily he would send her the bill, and then he left the farm. Emily glanced at Frank, as if taking in his khaki slacks and oxford shirt.

Noticing his bloody hands, she beckoned him over to a

room containing a sink and a large steel tank. After ripping off the long plastic gloves covering her hands and forearms and dropping them into the trash can, she turned the water on, pumped out several squirts of soap, and washed. "I thought you were the vet," she said, continuing to scrub her hands and forearms. "I've never met Dr. Lindsey's son, so that's why I assumed you were him." After rinsing, she pulled paper towels from a dispenser and gestured for Frank to use the sink.

Frank shrugged and walked to the sink, placing his hands under the running water. "Sorry. I helped you out, but I didn't have any idea if I was doing it right. It's probably good I showed up when I did. It looked like you'd been trying to help that cow for a long time."

She shook her head. "Cows are tough. They can be in labor for hours before giving birth. When you came, I'd just started pulling the calf out with the rope." She continued to stare, frowning. "Well, if you're not Dr. Lindsey's son, then who are you?"

He offered his recently washed hand, glad the nauseous feeling had evaporated from his stomach. "I'm Franklin Reese, Certified Public Accountant."

≈

Emily ignored his hand, narrowing her eyes. "You're kidding!"

"Why would I kid about this?" He beckoned her over to his abandoned briefcase and slid the golden locks open, removing a sheaf of papers. He held the documents toward her. "It's all right here. You called us to come out here because you said you lost your bookkeeper and you needed somebody to show you how to properly do the accounting for your farm."

She shook her head, refusing to take the papers. Gritting her teeth, she recalled the countless arguments she'd had with her stepmother, Laura, during the last several weeks. "So, you're the accountant from Bryer's and Ridge Accounting Firm that just opened in Monkton?"

He nodded. "The main office is at the Inner Harbor. They just opened this new branch to service the Monkton farm community."

She folded her arms in front of her. "I didn't call you; my stepmother did." She failed to admit that she was totally against hiring the accountant.

"Look. . .what's your name?" His mouth hardened into a thin line, and she found it hard not to stare at his cocoa brown, long-lashed eyes.

"My name is Emily Cooper."

He still clutched the papers, looking bewildered. "Did you want to call the office and reschedule?" He gestured toward the barn. "I see you've had a rough morning, so you might not be in the mood to talk about your finances right now."

"Just give me a second, okay?" She stepped away, noting how the cool scent of his cologne wafted around her, teasing her nose. She removed her cell phone from her pocket and hit the speed dial to call Laura. Emily left her stepmother a message, clutching the phone and speaking in a low voice so that Franklin would not hear her. "Mom, I thought we'd agreed you wouldn't hire that accountant until we talked about it some more. He's here now, and I'm not sure what to do." She ended her message and placed her phone back into her pocket. She gazed at the silos in the distance, still wondering how to handle this situation. The heated arguments she'd had with Laura about hiring an accountant played in her mind like a broken record.

"Did you want me to leave and come back another time?"

She jumped when his deep voice sounded behind her. "What's the phone number for your firm?"

He held the papers toward her. She took the cream-colored stationery, noting the number on the top. She called and spoke with the secretary, who confirmed Franklin's appointment.

She snapped her phone shut, and he presented her with a

laminated ID card. "I usually show this as soon as I get to a new house. But since you were busy in the barn, my routine was messed up. Did you want to call the office back and reschedule?" he asked again.

Shaking her head, she figured it was wrong of her to go against Laura's wishes. "No, come on." She gestured toward the house, wiping sweat from her brow. They walked to her home, and she opened the door and entered the shaded, screened-in porch. Emily removed her barn boots and noticed dung stuck on his footwear.

"Oh no." She cringed, feeling bad about the mess on Franklin's shoes and clothing. After leaving her boots on the porch, she told him to remove his shoes. They entered the kitchen, and she showed him the bathroom in the hallway. "You can wash up in there. I have some spare clothes you can wear so I can wash your shirt and shoes." He nodded, entering the bathroom. She soon reappeared with an old shirt and shoes that belonged to her father. She heard the water running from behind the closed bathroom door, and she left the clothes in front of the room's entrance.

When he returned to the kitchen, a strange, funny feeling rushed through her when she saw him wearing her father's stuff. "I'll get started laundering your clothes, and I'll clean your shoes. When you leave today, I'll have everything done."

He waved her comment away. "Can you just show me where you keep your files?"

"They're in my father's office." She approached the closed door, hesitating before opening it. She took a deep breath, beckoning him to follow her into her dad's space. Her arms ached from pulling the calf earlier, and the effects of her sleepless night made her want to take a long nap. When Franklin stood beside her, she became aware of his height. He glanced around before focusing on the filing cabinet. "Do you know where your father keeps his P & L statements?"

Emily frowned, looking around the cluttered room. "His what?"

"You know, his profit and loss statements."

Emily shrugged, now wishing she wasn't so ignorant about bookkeeping. "I don't know."

"Okay. How about his tax returns? That'll be a good place for me to start." He gestured toward the cabinet. "Are his tax forms in the filing cabinet?"

Emily glanced around the room, feeling out of her element. "I'm not sure."

"You don't even know where your tax returns are?" She cringed as the exasperation in his voice settled around the room like dust.

Gritting her teeth, she glared at him. "No, I don't know." Wringing her hands, she gazed at the piles of paper scattered around the office.

"Why did you call us for our services if you don't know where the paperwork is?" He threw his hands up in the air. "I feel like I'm wasting my time here. You know we charge by the hour."

She snapped, whipping her head toward the newcomer. "I'm sorry! I don't know where anything is. You're welcome to look and charge us for your extra time!" Hot tears pricked her eyes, and she turned away, not wanting Franklin to see her cry. "I have chores to do in the barn." She turned and exited the house, welcoming the intense heat as she ran down the hill toward the barn.

❧

When she rushed out of the office, remorse flowed through Frank. He shook his head, wishing he had not gotten so testy with Emily. Perhaps her father or her stepmother would arrive soon and show him where everything was. His head pounded, so he removed a bottle of water and some acetaminophen from his briefcase and took the pills. He guzzled the water before he turned the computer on. However, he discovered he couldn't access any files without a password. He put on his reading glasses, continuing to glance through the documents in the office. He would need Emily's help with finding the proper paperwork.

He wondered if his sudden move to Baltimore County had been a mistake. Maybe he should call his boss and get him to send somebody else for this assignment. When he was wondering what to do next, Emily returned. Her eyes were red, and she looked tired.

She took a deep breath. "I'm sorry I lost my temper with you earlier." She shrugged, and his heart melted with compassion.

"I want to apologize, too. I have a quick temper, and when people call us for services and don't have the proper paperwork, I get a little upset." The urge to rub her shoulder and let her know everything would be okay rushed through him. However, the urge quickly disappeared. "Our admin is supposed to send a letter or an e-mail beforehand, confirming our appointment and letting you know what files you need to have ready."

She shrugged. "Either Laura got the letter and forgot to tell me, or your admin didn't send it."

"So you're not sure where your father keeps his financial statements?" He glanced around the office. "Is he around to show me where they're filed?"

She shook her head, and her eyes filled with tears. She looked away for a few seconds and then turned toward him, wiping her eyes. "My father passed away a couple of weeks ago."

His heart skipped a beat. "I'm sorry." Shame for his earlier behavior rippled through his tired body. "I didn't know."

"It's okay. I haven't been myself since he died. My step-mother's taken his death pretty hard, so she left a couple of days ago, and she's staying with her daughter in Florida until she feels better."

He frowned. "You don't know how long she'll be gone?"

She shook her head. "She already had this trip planned before Dad died. My dad and Laura usually go to visit her daughter every year at the same time. She should be gone at least a few weeks. I already left her a voice mail asking her to call me."

"Why do you object to getting financial advice for your farm?" When she remained silent, he popped his briefcase open and again looked at the documents. "In addition to basic bookkeeping advice, your stepmom also wanted to have your farm audited."

"Audited? Why? I thought that was something the IRS randomly did to check up on taxpayers' returns."

He frowned, placing the paperwork on the scarred desk. "That's true, but people can hire accountants to audit their business to make sure they're following GAAP."

"GAAP?"

"Generally accepted accounting principles. For a farm or ranch, people might also want to know the net worth of their business. For some reason, your stepmother might want to know these things since your father is gone and she's not used to doing the bookkeeping." He gestured toward the computer. "Do you mind giving me the password for your computer? It might help me get started. Maybe your dad scanned or saved the documents."

She sat in the leather office chair, and he watched her slender brown fingers tapping on the keyboard, noticing her extremely short nails. After typing the password, she vacated the chair, gesturing for him to sit. "Where do you want to start?" she asked.

She pulled up a seat beside him, and they discussed where her father may have stored his electronic documents. Wisps of her dark hair escaped from her ponytail and rested on her slender neck. Realizing that he was staring, he forced his thoughts back to the job they were doing. They located some of the documents, and she stood. "I have stuff to do in the barn."

"You're running this farm alone?"

She folded her arms in front of her. "Sort of. We do have a couple of teenage brothers who help us out. They live on the horse farm up the road, but they're not very responsible."

"They don't always show up for work?"

"No, they don't, and it's wearing me down." She gestured toward the computer. "Laura and I never knew much about the finances of the farm, so when Dad died, we knew we needed a little bit of help for the chores, but we didn't want to go overboard and hire more help than we could afford. Darren and Jeremy, our teenage hired help, agreed to take turns helping me each day with the milking. Since it's summer, they have free time, and they each have other part-time jobs. One of them works at the Wagon Wheel."

"The Wagon Wheel?"

"It's a restaurant around here."

Frank glanced at Emily, still trying hard not to stare. "Was one of them supposed to be here this morning?"

She narrowed her eyes. "You got it. When one of them doesn't show up and I confront them about it, Darren will always say he thought Jeremy was coming and Jeremy will always say he thought Darren was supposed to come." She shrugged. "One or the other comes often enough for it not to be a huge problem. That is, not until today. It really would have helped me a lot if one of them had shown up and helped me with the difficult birth." Frank silently agreed with her.

"Why didn't you want your stepmother to hire outside accounting help?" he asked again.

"I have my reasons." He assumed that was her way of saying it was none of his business. "But since you're here and my stepmother wants you here, then I guess you need to get started."

As she turned to leave, he stopped her with a comment. "Oh, I forgot to tell you earlier, I prefer to be called Frank."

Emily nodded. Once she left, he began going through her father's Excel spreadsheets.

He accessed Mr. Cooper's most current document and began doing his job. A few hours later, he frowned. The numbers did not look accurate, and he figured it would take him a long time to figure out the late Mr. Cooper's accounting methods.

two

At five o'clock that evening, Emily opened the gate of the stanchion-style barn, which doubled as their milking parlor, and let the cows into their stalls. The thirty large black-and-white animals stomped into the enclosure, each going into her space.

"Hey, Emily."

She grinned with relief when Jeremy Dawson approached.

"I'm glad you finally showed up. I just finished cleaning the equipment for the milking and gave the cows their feed." She'd already attached the mobile milking units to the pipes so they could start milking the cows.

The lanky, mocha-colored teen ran his fingers over his newly corn-rowed hair. "Didn't Darren come this morning?"

She folded her arms in front of her chest, frowning. "No. Your brother didn't show up."

"But I thought he was going to come."

"You boys really need to make up your schedule. I really needed you here today."

He followed her into the stalls. "Why, did something happen?"

"Yes, Casey had her calf, and it came out backward."

The young man winced. She put her gloves on and took out the white bucket of cleaning solution. He went into the back room to wash his hands then returned. "Did somebody help you?" he asked.

He put on his gloves, and she handed him an iodine-filled dipper. After pressing the dipper against the udders of the first four cows, they wiped the iodine off the udders with a clean cloth. Then they turned the vacuum on and attached the mobile milking units to the four cows. As the machines milked the bovines, Emily and Jeremy worked together, cleaning the teats and udders of the next group of bovines.

One of the cows in the next group was especially dirty, so Emily cleaned the udders with the iodine and water solution in the bucket before using the dipper. She then explained how she'd had to use a rope to get the calf out, and she mentioned that their new accountant arrived in time to help her.

They worked together, milking four cows at a time, moving the mobile units from cow to cow before reattaching the units to the milk pipes. Emily found that the rhythmic thumping of the machines and the gentle swish of the white liquid going through the clear pipes soothed her frazzled nerves.

"So, you hired an accountant?" asked Jeremy after unhooking one of the machines. Cats scurried around the barn as he moved the unit to the next cow. Jeremy turned the suction on and hooked the machine to the udders of the animal. Emily then sprayed the recently milked cows' udders with disinfectant.

She still felt torn about having an outside person doing their finances. Couldn't she and Laura try to figure out the book-keeping on their own? "Yes." She told him the name of the firm they were using.

He nodded. "Yeah, my mom and dad hired an accountant a couple of months ago."

"Really? Why?"

The teen shook his head. "I don't know. Something about the IRS and an audit or something." He shrugged. She made a mental note to ask Jeremy's mother about her experiences using an outside accountant the next time she saw her in church.

Jeremy continued to speak as he attached a machine to another cow. "You know, I heard my mama talking to somebody on the phone, and she said that you need to get married to get somebody to help you take care of your farm since your mother doesn't like farming and your daddy's gone."

Her mouth dropped open, staring at the young man. "Jeremy, you shouldn't be repeating your mother's conversations."

He shrugged. "She didn't tell me not to repeat what she said."

Blowing air through her lips, she prayerfully tried to suppress her anger at Jeremy's mom for spreading untrue gossip. She'd always assumed Laura didn't like farming as much as she and her dad did, but she'd never heard her say she didn't like farming at all. She wondered if Laura had confided to Jeremy's mother that she didn't like her husband's profession. She knew Laura would sometimes visit Jeremy's mother and they'd have coffee or they'd sometimes volunteer for the same ministries at church.

She further wondered why Jeremy's mother would even be talking about Emily's single status. Since her breakup with her fiancé a year ago, marriage was the last thing on her mind. At twenty-eight, she felt her life was fulfilled just running the farm and trying to glean a profit from her family's business.

Once the milking equipment was cleaned and the cows, beef cattle, and bull were fed, she told Jeremy he could leave and asked him to make sure either he or his brother arrived at five o'clock the following morning to help milk the cows.

Her stomach rumbled, and she returned to the house after two and a half hours of milking and feeding in the barn. She heard Frank still in her father's office, typing on the computer. She needed to take a shower but felt uncomfortable doing so since Frank was still in the house. Her stomach growled again, and she missed Laura's home cooking. After washing her face, she removed Frank's clothing from the dryer. She needed to return his clothes to him before heading out to get something to eat.

When she approached the office, she caught Frank gathering his things to leave. He placed his glasses into the holder before closing the golden clasps on his leather briefcase. "I'll probably be back sometime tomorrow if that's okay with you."

"That's fine." She held his clothes up. "Here are your clothes. I forgot to give them to you earlier."

"Thanks. Do you mind if I use your bathroom to change?"

"Of course not."

He soon returned to the office, sporting the clothes he had been wearing earlier. He gave her the borrowed clothes, and she made a mental note that she and Laura still needed to go through her father's things and decide what they needed to keep. She removed the keys from her purse and followed Frank onto the screen porch and locked the door. She got into her old, battered white pickup truck, and Frank unlocked the door to his burgundy Lexus. When Emily turned the key in the ignition, the engine sputtered, refusing to start. She repeated the gesture, pressing on the gas. The grinding turn of the engine filled the hot summer air before it sputtered and died. Laying her head on the steering wheel, she groaned. "Lord, please let this truck start."

Sweat rolled down her neck when she sat up, turning the key again. When the engine failed, Frank appeared in the open window of the truck. Relief flowed through her like warm honey when she realized he had not driven away yet. Funny sensations danced in her stomach when he stood close to the vehicle. "I can't get my truck to start."

He glanced at the pickup. "How old is this thing?"

"My dad purchased it about fifteen years ago." She gestured toward the hood. "Whenever we had a problem with it, I'd always pop the hood, and he could fix it."

"I'm not very good with fixing cars, but I'll take a look," he offered. She pushed the button to pop the hood. She got out of the truck and joined him, looking down at the engine. The wires and inner workings were foreign to her, and the longing for her dad whisked through her, making her wish he were still alive. She blinked the sudden tears away, again focusing on the engine.

Frank tinkered for a bit before closing the hood. "I think you'll need to get a tow truck."

"I was afraid of that." Blowing air through her lips, she returned to the cab of the truck to retrieve her purse.

"Did you want to call a tow truck?"

"The auto shop down in Monkton is closed." She looked at her watch. "I'm going to call them for a tow tomorrow. They usually close around seven o'clock."

"Don't you have AAA? They'll send a tow out immediately."

She shook her head. "I've never needed AAA since I had Dad and the auto repair shop in Monkton."

"Can I give you a lift?"

She clutched the strap of her purse. "I don't want to hold you up. I might be able to get Kelly or Christine to pick me up."

"Who are Kelly and Christine?"

"My best friends. But I think they're working late tonight."

He continued to look at her, pulling his car keys out of his pocket. "I don't mind dropping you off. Where were you going?"

"I was going to Michael's to get a sub."

"Who's Michael? Your boyfriend?"

She shook her head, wondering why he would ask if Michael was her boyfriend. "No, Michael's Pizza. It's on York Road here in Monkton." She checked her watch, and her stomach grumbled. "I'm starved, and since Mom's been gone, I haven't done much cooking. I've been eating out a lot." She shrugged. "I'm a lousy cook."

He gestured toward his car. "I don't mind dropping you off."

"Well, if you're sure." She followed him to his luxury car and got in. He started the motor and turned on the air conditioning. He pulled out of the gravel driveway, and cool air filled the car, bringing relief to her heated body. "Ah, air conditioning."

He chuckled as he turned a corner and increased the temperature of the air conditioner. "You act like air conditioning is a luxury."

"Sometimes I feel like it is. The air conditioning in our truck conked out a few years ago, and we never got it fixed."

"Don't you have your own car?"

"I've never been able to afford a new car. I had a used one for years, but it stopped working a month ago, and with Dad's death and everything, I haven't had time to try and replace it."

They soon pulled into the parking lot of the small strip mall where Michael's Pizza was located. She exited the car, surprised when Frank cut the ignition and got out of the vehicle. "I hope you don't mind my eating with you. I wanted to talk to you about the little bit you may know about the finances on your farm. Besides, you'll need somebody to drop you off after you eat." He retrieved his briefcase from the backseat, and when she glanced at the floor, she noticed some liquor bottles. She frowned, and he dropped the briefcase back onto the seat. "Would you prefer that I not eat with you?"

She shook her head, putting the image of the liquor from her mind, knowing it was none of her business. "No, I'm okay with it."

He retrieved his briefcase before they entered the establishment. Tomatoes, garlic, and cheese scented the air, and Emily's mouth watered as she sat at one of the two tables located in the carryout restaurant. "Do you mind if we split a pizza?" asked Frank.

She told him she didn't mind, and Frank went to the counter and returned with two Cokes. "They said the pizza will be ready in about twenty minutes. I ordered pepperoni and extra cheese with mushrooms. Is that okay?"

"That sounds good."

A group of rowdy teenagers entered and sat at the table across from them. At first it was hard to talk, but the owner came over and told the teenagers to hold the noise down. When the ruckus stopped, she expressed her concerns about her farm. "I've been calling my mom all day. I think she's avoiding me."

"Why would she avoid you?"

She sipped her drink. "Laura has never been the most straightforward person. She beats around the bush about things and expects you to figure stuff out yourself. It drives me nuts."

"You told me earlier that she was your stepmother. You two must be pretty close if you call her Mom."

Emily nodded. "Sometimes I call her Mom. We're kind of close. My dad married Laura ten years ago, right before I graduated from high school." She shook her head, not wanting to discuss the somewhat complicated relationship she shared with her stepmother. "Believe me, I didn't start calling her Mom right away."

He opened his briefcase and removed a stack of paper before placing his reading glasses over his caramel eyes. She watched him flip through the papers, her curiosity about him sprouting like a geyser. He looked up and caught her staring. She looked away, wanting to put this whole situation into perspective. "What did you want to talk to me about?"

"Number one, I just want you to know that it's going to take me a long time, probably a week or more, to complete the audit for your farm. It'll be costly, but we have payment plans, and Laura has already signed the agreement."

"That figures," she mumbled. "She agrees to your services and doesn't tell me a thing."

He continued to flip through his papers. "I've already accessed a great deal of your father's files, and I think I can help advise you and your mom about budgeting, forecasting, and doing the bookkeeping on your farm." He looked at her, and her heart pounded from his intense gaze. "What I need from you is a description about where all of your revenue comes from. I know you get revenue from the milk, but where else do you get revenue? I just want to be sure your father has everything covered in all his files."

Emily started talking about where money flowed into their

farm—from cows, beef cattle, heifers, and crops.

He interrupted her. "So, you have cash crops as well as crops you grow for feed?"

"We sure do. We've always done this, because it's hard to make a living from such a small herd of cows. We usually just plant extra so we'll have some left over to sell."

He continued to write, nodding. "I understand. A lot of smaller dairy farms must have some cash crops to survive."

She explained how they hired outside help to assist with harvesting their crops.

He scanned his notes. "Are there any other sources of income?"

"No." She thought about it for a few seconds, figuring she had covered all of their revenue sources. Then she grabbed his arm. "Oh! I forgot about one thing! It's not a source of income directly from the farm, but it does help out."

Frank flipped to a fresh sheet of paper, encouraging her to continue.

"Well, my mom's back went out on her a few years ago. So bending over, milking the cows, and doing manual labor on the farm just wasn't agreeing with her anymore. Since she didn't work on the farm any longer for health reasons, she got a job down at the elementary school. She works in the cafeteria. She loves being around the kids, and she said the work isn't as intense as farming. Since the school is closed during the summer, she's free to do other things." Emily continued to talk nonstop about the farm for twenty minutes, and Frank took notes. She talked about her cows, telling him their names and describing their personalities.

"You name your cows? I've never seen a farmer do that."

"I don't name all of them, but I name my favorite ones." She explained that she had them trained to go into the same stall each night and that most of the larger farms didn't have such a personal relationship with their animals. Their pizza arrived, but she didn't touch it until she'd finished answering Frank's questions. He removed his reading glasses before he took the spatula and served thin slices of gooey, cheesy pizza onto the paper plates. Emily bowed her head, saying grace over her meal. She noticed that Frank respectfully waited until she finished before he bit his pizza.

She tasted her food, savoring the spices and the tangy pepperoni. "This is so good."

"It's doesn't beat Chicago-style pizza. That's where I'm from."

"You're from Chicago?"

He nodded, sipping his soda. "Yes, born and raised there. That's where my family lives." His cell phone rang. He excused himself as he took the call. "Hey, sport! Did you guys win the game?" A smile brightened his face as he listened to the other person on the line. "Yes, I remember. What happened after you pitched?" The conversation continued for a few minutes before Frank said he was with a client and had to go. He promised to call back the following day.

He flipped his phone shut and placed it in his briefcase.

"Was that your son?"

Frank shook his head. "That was my nephew, Mark." He frowned and stared at the pizza for a few seconds. "My sister has two kids, and she's been having a rough time with them since her husband left her for another woman a year ago."

"That's awful."

"It's been pretty bad, so I made a point to spend a lot of time with the kids after their dad left." He shrugged as he took another slice of pizza. "I feel that every kid needs to have a dad, and I want to be there for them since their father doesn't appear to have time for them anymore."

They ate in silence for a few minutes before Emily asked another question. "How long have you lived in Maryland?"

"I've only been here a few days."

"Really?"

He nodded. "I relocated here from Chicago."

"Why?"

"It was hard for me to leave my niece and nephew, but a lot has happened, and I just felt like I needed a change. Do you ever feel that way?"

"Not really."

"Well, I did." He finished his slice of pizza and removed another piece from the box. "The accounting firm in the Inner Harbor was expanding, and they opened the branch in Monkton to serve the farming community. Since they recently expanded into farm and ranch accounting, they needed somebody to temporarily head up that new division. One of the perks they offer to customers that many of the other farm and ranch accounting places don't offer is door-to-door service. That's why I came directly to your farm. Some accounting places require farmers to bring their files into their office."

"So you're only here temporarily?"

He shrugged. "I'm not sure. I didn't want to commit to stay long-term until I decided if I liked it here or not. So they said we could play it by ear and see what happens. I work at the office in Monkton, but I also have to go to the main office in the Inner Harbor sometimes, too. I rented an apartment not far from the Inner Harbor."

"So, when they needed somebody, you volunteered?"

He shook his head. "Not initially. They came to me and asked me to do it, and I had to think about it for a bit before deciding to come. I had to get licensed to practice in the state of Maryland before I was able to make the move out here."

She frowned, wondering if he was the right person to be showing them their bookkeeping. "What do you know about farm and ranch accounting since your company just recently started offering it to clients?"

"We have a farm and ranch division in Illinois. I advised a lot of farmers located in rural areas on the outskirts of Chicago. I'll admit you're the first client I've served via the door-to-door service. That's not something we offered in Illinois, but they're going to start offering that soon in that state also." He changed the subject. "You've always lived on your family's dairy farm?"

She nodded, helping herself to more pizza. "I have one sister and two stepsisters. My sister, Sarah, hated farming. She left the farm when she was still in her early twenties. She lives in Idaho." She sipped her soda. "My stepsister Lisa lives in Florida, and Laura is visiting her right now. My other stepsister, Becky, is pregnant, and she lives in California. It's a difficult, high-risk pregnancy, and it's a shame she couldn't come to my father's funeral."

"Is this her first child?" Frank took another slice of pizza and sprinkled red pepper flakes on it. His leg jiggled beneath the table, and she wondered if he was nervous.

"No, she has two more, and she's really struggling right now. She's a stay-at-home mom, and her husband works full-time. Since her pregnancy has been so difficult and she is supposed to take it easy, a lot of people from her church have been helping her out."

"It sounds like you're close to your stepsisters."

Emily shook her head. "We're not really that close. I've seen them off and on since my dad married Laura. I'm not as close to them as I am to Sarah."

They ate in silence for a few minutes before Frank asked another question. "Why are you so against your mother hiring an accountant? You never answered me earlier."

She sighed. "This is a family business, and you are not family. When Dad died, I wanted to try and figure out the bookkeeping myself, and I wanted my stepmother to help, but we kept arguing about it. I asked her if she'd at least wait for a couple of months to give me some time to go through Daddy's files."

"And she didn't agree to do that?" he guessed.

"I guess not, because she's gone and you're here."

"Well, your attitude is not very smart."

She frowned. "Why do you say that?"

He folded his arms in front of him, his leg continuing to jiggle. "Emily, you just admitted that you know nothing about the way your father accounted for the profits to your farm. You need an accountant to help you figure things out. You certainly don't want to be flagged for an audit by the IRS. If you are, it'll make things more difficult if you don't know what you're doing."

Pressing her lips together, she looked toward the counter. He touched her hand. "Hey, don't get offended. I just don't think you've thought through this very clearly."

"Whatever," she mumbled, draining her soda cup.

He chuckled, gazing at the empty pizza box. "I guess we had big appetites tonight."

"I tend to eat a lot of food."

"Do you?"

He seemed surprised, so she explained. "I've always eaten a lot of food, because doing those farm chores every day works up an appetite."

"You can't tell that you have a big appetite by looking at you," Frank said before he finished his soda.

Once he'd gathered his papers and placed them back into his briefcase, he closed it and paid the bill before they returned to his car. After he turned on the air conditioning, she rummaged through her purse. "I can pay for half the pizza."

"It's just a pizza. Besides, I can expense the meal since we were talking about business most of the time, anyway." When they pulled into the dairy farm, he reminded her that he would be returning the following day.

After she had showered and gotten ready for bed, she was about to open her Bible when her phone rang. "Hello?"

"Hi, Emily."

"Kelly, hi. What's up?"

Her best friend told her about the date she was looking forward to. "I can't wait to see Martin again."

When Kelly continued to speak, Emily struggled to listen as fatigue washed over her entire body like a tidal wave. "Did you call just to talk about Martin?"

"No. I was wondering if you wanted to go shopping with me next Saturday. I'm going to get my hair and nails done; then I'm going to look for a new outfit for my date Saturday night."

Emily lay back on her pillows, thinking about how busy she was the following weekend. "I want to go to the livestock auction. Is Christine going shopping with you?"

"I'd ask her, but I don't think it's a good idea."

"Why not?"

"Do you have to ask? Christine loves shopping a bit too much. She admitted that if she doesn't curb her compulsive shopping habit, she'll never be able to get rid of all her debt."

"She just needs to find something else to do in her spare time besides shopping." Emily changed the subject. "How are things over at the bank?" She struggled to listen but had a hard time staying awake. She thought about her crazy day, and her fatigue lifted for a few seconds when her brain focused on other things. Emily told Kelly about the difficult birth and about Frank showing up to help her. She then talked about the meeting she'd had with him at the pizza parlor.

"Oh, Em, it sounds like you had a very stressful day."

"Yes, I just don't know what to do."

"What can you do? Your stepmother is still in charge of the farm. Isn't she the official owner since your dad died?"

"Sort of. Dad's will made her the owner of a larger percentage, but part of this farm is mine. That's why I wish she had told me she'd hired an accountant to look at the books."

"Em, you need to let go a bit. You can't do everything by yourself. When your dad died, Laura had to argue with you about hiring Jeremy and Darren to help with the milking."

"My dad and I always did the milking together."

Kelly's sigh carried over the wire. "But your dad's not here anymore, Em, and you need help."

Tears rushed to Emily's eyes, and she wiped them away. Sniffing, she grabbed a tissue. Kelly was silent for a few moments before continuing. "Have you talked to your stepmom today?"

"No, she didn't call me back."

Kelly spoke again. "When you were telling me about Frank, you sounded a little excited. Is he cute?"

Emily threw her soiled tissues into the trash can beside her bed. "Yes!" She recalled Frank's physical attributes. "He's got medium brown skin, and he's really tall, taller than me. He's got these nice brown eyes with long lashes, and he wears the best-smelling cologne. When I'm around him, it's kind of hard for me to stay focused."

"Sounds like you're interested in him."

"No, I failed to mention that I saw some liquor bottles in his backseat." She thought about it for a few minutes. "We mostly talked about the farm, and I told him about the revenue that flowed in, and he wanted to know the cycles for the crops and about last year's selling prices." She mentioned what he'd told her about his sister's husband and her children.

"Did you have a good time talking to him?"

"It wasn't a bad time, but. . .I don't know. I sensed he was nervous or something. His leg kept jiggling under the table."

"Maybe he likes you."

"I doubt it."

"How old is he?"

"I'm not sure. I think he might be a little bit older than me."

They talked about Frank for a few more minutes before Emily yawned. "I think I'm going to sleep right now. Are you getting ready to go to bed?"

Before Kelly could comment, her other line clicked. "Kelly, I've got to go. That might be Mom calling me back." Kelly said good-bye before Emily clicked to the other line. "Hello?"

"Emily, it's me."

"Mom! What took you so long to call me back?"

"I wanted to give you a chance to cool down before I called. I knew you'd be upset about me hiring that accountant."

Emily huffed, and her fatigue evaporated, replaced with anger. "Why did you hire him without asking me first?"

"I did ask you, but all you wanted to do was argue about it. I felt justified to overstep your wishes since you don't always know what's best. You're just as stubborn as your father, and I didn't think you'd ever listen to reason, so that's why I signed the paperwork so the accountant could show you what to do."

Emily gritted her teeth, still struggling to calm down. She closed her eyes, silently praying for strength. She decided to change the subject since there was nothing she could do about Laura's hiring Frank. "How is Lisa doing?"

Laura groaned. "Not too good. She broke up with her boyfriend right before Paul died, and now all she does is go to work and then come home to mope around." Once she'd talked about Lisa, she said that Becky was still doing about as well as could be expected with her pregnancy. Emily had wondered why Laura would visit Lisa so long when Becky seemed to need her more. She was practically on bed rest. When Emily had asked Laura about it, Laura had sadly told her that she didn't think Becky wanted her to come for an extended visit.

"Mom, Frank will be back tomorrow. We'll probably place you on a conference call so you'll know what's going on."

"Thanks, Emily. I appreciate that." Emily said good-bye to Laura before hanging up the phone, curling beneath the blankets, and drifting to sleep.

three

Following the forty-minute drive from Monkton, Frank cruised down Pratt Street near the Inner Harbor. He barely paid attention to the throngs of people walking the sidewalks on the warm summer night. The blue electric wave decorating the Baltimore Aquarium blazed in the darkness, and he sighed, anxious to get to his recently rented apartment in the heart of Baltimore.

Once he'd parked, he opened the door to his backseat and removed the glass bottles filled with liquor. He sighed, riding the elevator to his loft apartment. After unlocking the door, he threw his briefcase onto the couch, opened the refrigerator, and pulled out a club soda. He placed several ice cubes into the plastic tumbler. He then poured a little soda over the ice before pouring a healthy amount of his favorite imported scotch into the container. Sitting on the couch, he sipped his drink, his frazzled nerves slowly calming after he'd drunk half the amount in the glass.

The nervous twitch in his leg stopped when he settled into his nighttime routine. He lifted the remote, turning on the network news, thinking about his weird day. When his boss suggested he take the Cooper client, he felt it was just what he needed.

It turned out he was wrong.

When Emily was around him, he couldn't stay focused. The spark of delight that shined in her eyes when she spoke of her farm warmed his heart. He continued to nurse his drink. Her long dark hair and creamy brown complexion made it hard for him to concentrate on his work.

Before they'd gone into Michael's Pizza for dinner, he noticed her frown when she saw the booze in his car. He'd also noticed that she prayed for her meal before she ate. He shook his head. Emily reminded him so much of Julie that it was scary.

His thoughts continued to wander as he entered the kitchen and fixed another drink. When he returned to the couch, he lifted his wedding photo, touching Julie's face, again wondering when he would get over the pain of losing his wife. Taking sip after sip, his mind grew fuzzy as the alcohol chased away the demons that haunted him.

છ

During the next few days working on Emily's farm, Frank tried hard to ignore his attraction to her. She patiently answered his questions about the farm, providing necessary information he needed to do his job. They called her stepmother via speakerphone, and he consulted with Laura about what he planned on doing about the bookkeeping and the audit. He told the older woman he'd be doing the audit for at least a week or more, and she seemed to accept his presence in her home. He still wondered if his attraction to Emily was a good thing. Thoughts of Julie still hovered in his mind, and Emily was the first person he had met who could make him forget about his wife for hours at a time.

છ

When Frank opened his eyes the following Saturday morning, his head felt like it was going to explode. He checked the bedside clock, glad that it was still early, only six thirty. Once he drank a few cups of black coffee, he would feel ready to go into the office before heading out to Emily's farm. His boss was always hounding him about working too many overtime hours on the weekends, but Frank found he enjoyed working more than being alone in his apartment. Working long hours helped make his mind too tired to dwell on the problems he struggled to forget. His cell phone chirped. He lifted the small black instrument from his nightstand and groaned when he saw his sister's phone number displayed in the caller ID window. He closed his eyes and sighed for a few seconds before answering the call. "What is it, Trish?"

"Good morning to you, too, little brother. I should have had Mark call you from his cell phone instead. You seem happier talking to my children than to me."

He lay back on the pillow, trying to relieve his throbbing headache and ignoring her apt observation. "Do you realize it's six thirty in the morning?"

"Yes, but I've been calling you since you moved to Baltimore, and you never answer your phone, yet you always answer when Mark calls. I figured if I called you early enough, you'd at least think it was an emergency."

He rubbed his eyes. "Is there an emergency?"

She hesitated. "Yes."

"Yeah, I'll bet there is." Sarcasm filled his voice. "What's the emergency?"

"Mom's been pretty upset since you left."

"I've been pretty upset since she rejected my wife." His sister sighed, and he struggled to control his temper. "What does Mom want me to do?"

"She wants you to start talking to her and Dad again. Julie's dead now and—"

"Just because Julie's dead means I need to forget what they've done?"

"But it's been over a year. Don't you think it's time to move on?"

"No, I don't," he grunted. "Look, my head hurts, and I don't feel like talking about this right now."

She ignored his comment. "Dad hasn't been feeling well."

He sat up in bed, his stomach churning from the sudden movement. He calmed himself down before asking, "Is he okay?"

"See, I know you still care."

He ignored the comment. "Is Dad okay?" he repeated.

"He's been complaining a lot about having a headache, and Mom says he's hardly eating."

"What does the doctor say?"

She sighed, her voice wavering. "He refuses to go to the doctor." The siblings were silent for a few seconds before Trish spoke again. "I think Dad's guilt about what happened is eating away at him."

He gritted his teeth. "Trish, you know they were wrong! You finally became friends with Julie. You know how much I loved her. . . . You know why I loved her."

"I loved Julie, too."

"I know you did. She always told me if she were to have a sister, she'd want her to be just like you."

"I know. That's why you really need to get over yourself and stop running away from your problems."

"I'm not running away—"

"But you are. Don't you get it?"

"No, I don't know what you're talking about."

"Yes, you do. I'll bet you're still having nightmares about Julie's death, and you probably have a headache because you got drunk last night."

Frank winced at the truth of his sister's words, refusing to confirm her suspicions. "I'm dealing with it the only way I know."

"Well, you need to find another way to deal with your pain. Alcohol and nightmares are doing nothing to help you."

"Well, what do you suggest I do?"

"If I told you, you wouldn't want to hear it."

"Try me."

"Why don't you do what Julie would have wanted you to do? Why don't you give God a chance? Since Julie led me to the Lord, I've found it so much easier to deal with my problems."

"I don't see how you can talk about trusting the Lord. Your husband left you! Look at all the problems you've been having with Mark and Regina since he left."

"It's been hard, but I'm trying to teach my kids that even though their earthly father is not around much anymore, they have a heavenly Father who loves them and will never leave them." He remained silent. "You might want to give God a try and let Him help you with all that you're dealing with. Another thing you might want to do is not be so angry at Mom and Dad."

"Wait a minute."

"No, you wait a minute. Just hear me out about this. I know Mom and Dad didn't like Julie because she didn't come from a good family, and it was wrong of them to think like that. But you have to remember that money's been in our family for decades, and Mom and Dad have been raised to think this way. It's wrong, but in their own twisted way, they felt this was one way to show their love for us: making sure we chose an appropriate mate from a prestigious family."

He was speechless, unsure of how to respond to his sister's comment. Before he could say anything, she changed the subject. "You'll never guess who I saw at the grocery store yesterday."

"Who?"

"Brian. He said a lot of the kids at the rec center still ask about you, and I told him that you'd moved to Baltimore." She sighed. "You've been so sad and bitter since Julie died. You used to be so happy spending your free time at the rec center helping Brian mentor those teenagers. I remember how you used to look forward to having some kids of your own."

He swallowed, tears rushing to his eyes as he recalled the happier times in his life.

"Look, I have to go now. I need to start making breakfast for the kids. I just wanted you to think about what I've told you and to try and talk to Mom and Dad again."

He wiped his eyes and grunted before he ended the call, not wanting to discuss the matter further. He got out of bed and took some acetaminophen. His stomach still roiled when he made his way to the kitchen. He measured dark grinds into the filter, and the fragrant scent of coffee soon filled the air. Taking a mug from the cupboard, he filled it with his morning brew, sat at a chair in the kitchen, and thought about Trish's advice. He just wasn't ready to forgive his parents for what they'd done—he just couldn't.

A few hours later he dressed and called Emily. He was surprised when she answered on the first ring. "Hi, I thought you would be out milking the cows."

"I'm finished with that already. I do it at five a.m."

He chuckled. "Actually, I was awake at six thirty this morning."

"Really?"

He sensed she was going to say something else, but when she remained silent, he continued. "Look, I know it's Saturday, but I wanted to know if it was okay if I came to your farm for a few hours today. I need to go to the auction—"

"You're going to the auction over in Westminster?"

"Yes, I was going to head over there because my boss said it was a good idea to see what the livestock are selling for. I agreed to go, so after I do that, I thought I could spend a few hours on your father's files."

"Could I ask a huge favor of you?"

"What's up?"

"Could you pick me up for the auction? My truck is still in the shop, and I didn't want to spend money on a rental. I borrowed a truck from another farmer for a few days to run some errands, but the garage said my vehicle is still not fixed."

Her apprehensive tone made him wonder if she rarely asked others for favors. "I don't mind picking you up. Are you planning on adding to your herd?"

"No, I'm going for another reason. I'll explain when you get here."

He said good-bye and hung up the phone.

A few minutes later he exited his apartment building and stopped as a woman walked by. The ivory suit and high heels reminded him of one of Julie's favorite outfits. The female had a surety to her step as she sauntered by, and Frank felt frozen in time when he watched her.

The woman's dark eyes widened as he stared. "I'm sorry, I thought you were somebody else," he explained, ashamed to be caught staring at a woman who resembled his wife. She frowned and walked away. Frank leaned against his apartment building, the bright sun shining in his eyes. That was the third time since Julie's death that he'd made this error. He closed his eyes, wondering when he'd learn to accept that his wife was dead and move on with his life.

He shook his head, strolling to the small parking lot. Once he got into his vehicle, he stared out the window. Maybe spending the day with Emily at an auction was what he needed to get his mind off his nightmares.

❧

Emily tried to relax the kink in her shoulders, hurrying to get dressed before Frank arrived. Fatigue rushed through her like a tidal wave. She really wanted to take a morning nap, but she wanted to go to the auction today. A knock sounded, and her heart rushed with excitement when she ran to the door and opened it. "Oh, hi." She tried not to let her disappointment show when Cameron, the milk truck driver, entered the kitchen.

"Hi, Emily. I've already put your milk in the tank. I just stopped in to say hello."

She tried to smile. "Hi, Cam."

He continued to look at her. "You look real nice this

morning." He crumpled his baseball cap between his thick, dark fingers. She knew he was just trying to flatter her. Emily sensed Cameron staring when she poured a glass of water.

She gulped her beverage before placing the glass in the sink.

He grabbed the back of a chair and pulled it away from the table. Gesturing toward the seat, he said, "You look like you could use a rest."

Cameron's hands trembled. He wasn't a bad-looking man, but she wished he wouldn't stay around so much. If he wasn't so nervous, she could imagine a host of eligible women flocking to the milk truck driver.

Emily poured a cup of coffee and sat in the offered chair. "Would you like some coffee?"

He shook his head. "No thanks. I'm going to be leaving soon anyway." He frowned. "You look tired. Is something wrong?" Concern filled his voice.

She clutched the coffee mug, closing her eyes briefly. "No, nothing's wrong." She took another sip of coffee. "I don't mean to keep you from getting to your next milk pickup," she began, anxious for Cameron to take his exit so she could leave with Frank when he arrived. She glanced at the screen door, and her heart skipped a beat when she saw Frank standing on the porch. "Hi." Her throat was suddenly dry, and she sipped from her mug of coffee when Frank entered the kitchen. The cool scent of his aftershave filled the room with musky sweetness, and she sighed, relishing his presence in her home.

During the last week, Frank had appeared torn about his decision to relocate from Chicago to Baltimore. He'd told her that his nephew called him every day, saying he wished Frank had not left. He regretted missing Mark's Little League games, and since he'd left, his sister, Trish, said that Mark had started misbehaving again. Frank had mentioned that he planned to take a weekend and visit Trish and her children soon and that he was still angry that Trish's husband had abandoned their family a year ago.

Emily found it heartwarming that Frank wanted to be a substitute parent to Trish's children. Whenever he spoke of his niece and nephew, his face brightened, and when Mark called him periodically, Frank immediately dropped what he was doing to see what his nephew wanted to talk about.

She'd been working closely with Frank this week as they went over her father's accounting records. Whenever he looked at her, she became flustered, her heart racing like a horse speeding out to pasture. She couldn't seem to keep Frank from dominating her thoughts—or tempting her heart.

"Good morning, Emily." When he came toward her, she immediately noticed his cocoa brown eyes were red and his mouth was set in a firm line, as if he were angry. He sported a simple white T-shirt and jeans, and the material of his shirt hugged his broad shoulders. Frank's dark eyes were full of curiosity as he gazed at Cameron.

Frank offered his hand. "I'm Frank."

Cameron still clutched his baseball cap in his left hand when the two men shook hands. "I'm Cameron Jacobs." His deep voice wavered, and Emily wondered when he was going to leave. She was sure he was due to the next farm for pickup by now.

Cameron placed his hat on his head. "Well, I'd better get going. Take care of yourself, Emily, and I'll see you in a couple of days." The screen door banged shut when he left.

Frank drew his brows together, glaring at Cameron as he walked toward his milk truck. "Is he your boyfriend?" He sat at the table, still looking at her with those intense eyes. Emily sipped from her coffee cup, refusing to let his presence unnerve her.

"He's been asking me out for over a year."

"I can tell he likes you. You've never gone out with him?"

She shrugged, again wondering why she couldn't control her emotions. Her attraction to Frank was strong, stronger than what she'd ever felt for Cameron, yet Cameron was a Christian and they shared the same passionate faith in God. Why couldn't she feel physically attracted to Cameron?

She finished her coffee and went to the cupboard to get a box of cereal. She poured cornflakes into a large bowl then gestured toward the box. "Did you want some cereal?"

He shook his head and touched his stomach. "I don't want any breakfast this morning."

She peered at him again, and he squirmed beneath her intense gaze. "Your eyes are red."

He sighed, scooting his chair back. "I don't feel well this morning."

She let the subject drop, adding milk and banana to her cereal. She dipped her spoon into the bowl, and he waited a few minutes before speaking. "So, why are you going to the auction today if you're not planning on purchasing any cows?"

In between large bites of cereal, she explained. "My father and I used to go to the auction as a social outlet. We'd talk to other farmers, look at the animals being auctioned off—that sort of thing. Sometimes we'd sell our beef cattle there, but I don't have one that's old enough to sell right now." She stopped eating, gathering her thoughts. "We'd already planned to go today. . .before he passed. And I just want to go because I like going."

When she finished her cereal, she drank the last of the milk from the bowl, and Frank chuckled, gazing at her fondly. "That's the biggest bowl of cereal I've ever seen a woman eat."

She smiled back. "I told you milking those cows every morning and doing chores makes me work up an appetite."

"Did your farm help come this morning?" he asked before she rinsed out her cereal bowl and placed it in the dishwasher.

She nodded. "Yes, one of them did show up, and that was

great. They've been doing pretty good since Casey had her calf." When she was finished in the kitchen, she went to her bedroom to get her purse. "Are you ready to go?" she asked as she removed her keys from her handbag. Frank nodded, and she locked the door before they headed to his vehicle.

After they were settled in his car, he turned the air conditioning up as he pulled away from the house. "You'll need to tell me where to go since I left the directions at my apartment." She settled into the leather seat, taking pleasure in the cool air. "Do you know when they're going to get your truck repaired?"

"They had to order some parts. It shouldn't be too much longer before it's fixed. Probably next week sometime." When he stopped at a light, he removed a pair of shades from his glove compartment. He placed his sunglasses over his eyes. "Did your mom ever tell you why she hired me without asking you first?"

Emily sighed, folding her arms in front of her. "Yes." She briefly explained what had been said during the conversation she'd had with Laura after Frank's first day on the farm.

He glanced at her before pulling away from the light. "Do you believe her?"

She shrugged. "I don't know. My stepmother is certainly not prone to lying. She does seem to overstep her boundaries sometimes, though. This should have been a decision we made together." She looked out the window, frowning. "Since my daddy died, I don't know what to believe anymore."

"What do you mean?"

"Nothing is the same. You know, when somebody you love is alive, you just take the days for granted, thinking you'll see them the next day. Now that my daddy's dead, my stepmother hasn't been the same—I haven't been the same. I can't sleep, she can't sleep, and the only solace I seem to find is working with the cows and reading my Bible."

"If God is so almighty, then why does He allow people to suffer so much?" The question startled her.

"I don't know, but my belief in Him and knowing my dad is in heaven gives me some comfort."

He changed the subject. "Is that all your mother said?"

"Pretty much. I've spoken to her a few times since you've started the audit. Ever since she's been in Florida with her daughter, she sounds better, happier. I almost feel like she doesn't want to come home."

"Do you still think she's only going to stay for a few weeks?"

"It's hard to say. The elementary school is closed for the summer, so I guess she's not in a hurry to come home."

"I see. Is that all she said?"

She watched him carefully. "Is there something wrong?"

Tension knotted her muscles when she noticed he clutched the steering wheel. "It's still early in the audit process. Your father's budget looks good, but I can't tell you about the financial solvency of your farm until I've completed the audit." He sighed when he stopped at another light. "I just found out something interesting yesterday that I thought you should know. I figured your mom would've told you when she called, but she obviously didn't."

"What are you talking about?"

The car behind them honked, prompting them to drive since the light had changed. He quickly turned left onto Highway 137 before responding to her question. "I was looking through your father's computer files, and I found a spreadsheet that he called Estimated Selling Cost. I also found some correspondence he had with a Realtor."

"A Realtor? What Realtor?"

Frank shrugged. "There wasn't a name or address, but it looked like he was drafting a letter or e-mail to a property sales-man. The spreadsheet listed properties that were recently sold in the Baltimore County area that were similar to your farm."

"Why would my dad be in contact with a Realtor?"

Frank shrugged. "It's hard to say, but from looking at the files, it appears as if he was thinking about selling your property."

Her heart skipped a beat. "Are you sure?"

He kept one hand on the steering wheel and touched her arm with the other. In spite of her shock, her skin tingled. He shook his head. "No, I'm not sure. I'm only speculating. I can show you what I found if you'd like." Silence filled the car. "Are you okay?"

She toyed with her ponytail. "I can't believe my dad would even think about selling our farm."

"He might not have been trying to sell. I'm only speculating."

Emily breathed deeply, trying to digest this new information.

"Where do I turn?" he asked when they entered a roundabout.

She told him to make a right at the first road. He sighed, taking the first exit. The information about her father sat in her brain like a twisted knot, waiting to be untangled. She definitely needed to speak with her stepmother again.

She watched the passing scenery. "I don't understand why Laura didn't tell me all this."

"Maybe she didn't know." He glanced at her with concern. "Are you okay?"

"No, I'm upset about this news." Her life suddenly seemed to be speeding out of control, and she wondered what other secrets her father may have been harboring.

four

When the livestock auction was finished, people cleared out of the enclosure, and Frank touched Emily's elbow as they walked to the car. It was almost dinnertime. "I guess you need to be getting home to milk the cows?"

"Both of the brothers are supposed to come tonight for the milking."

"Did you want to get a bite to eat? I know how much you hate cooking." He opened her door for her, and they settled into his vehicle.

She bit her lower lip, staring out the windshield. "Frank, I don't know—"

"I wanted to talk to you about something."

"Can't we talk about it now?"

"Well, you're hungry, aren't you?"

She nodded, a small smile teasing her full lips. The urge to kiss her flowed through him, and he had to make a conscious effort to ignore the romantic feelings that drifted inside his mind.

"Of course I'm hungry," she said.

"Then let's get something to eat."

"Okay. Let me call Jeremy and Darren to make sure they're doing the milking right now." Once she called and confirmed that both brothers had shown up at her farm and were milking the cows, he drove them downtown to the Inner Harbor in Baltimore. After he parked in a garage, they entered the trendy tourist district. "Do you want to eat at the Cheesecake Factory?"

She nodded as they approached the high-class restaurant.

Noise filtered from the dining crowd. When they approached the hostess, she gave them a pager and placed their names on a list. "There's an hour wait," she said above the noise. "We'll page you when the table is ready. Just be sure you don't go too far away."

"A whole hour?" asked Emily.

The hostess shrugged. "We're always busy on Saturday evenings."

Frank took the pager, and they strolled around the Inner Harbor. The breeze blew over the water, and he invited Emily to sit on a bench. Boats bobbed on the Chesapeake Bay, and throngs of people walked by, many carrying bags of purchases from the shops in Harborplace. A jazz saxophonist played his horn, and several people dropped money into his instrument case. The music surrounded them, the mellow notes filling the air.

She tilted her head back, closing her eyes. "It sure is nice out here." The hot wind blew her ponytail, and jealousy filled his soul when several men walked by, giving Emily a second glance.

"Yes, it is nice. Do you come here often?"

She shook her head. "Not much. Sometimes my friends and I come out here for dinner. But we haven't done that in months."

They sat in companionable silence, and he was tempted to hold her hand. But he resisted, unsure if she would want him to. The red lights on the pager brightened when the instrument buzzed. "I guess our table is ready," he said.

ষ

Emily's stomach rumbled with hunger. Their server approached. "My name is Allen, and I'll be your server tonight. What can I get you all to drink?"

Frank's leg was twitching, and she again wondered if her presence made him nervous. He ordered first. "I'll have a Coke."

She ordered lemonade and a glass of water. Allen soon reappeared, prompting them to place their food orders. "I'll have the Cajun jambalaya pasta," said Emily.

Once Frank had ordered the Jamaican black pepper shrimp, she voiced her concerns about her father. "Do you really think my father would want to sell his farm?"

He looked at her, frowning. "Are you sure you don't want to talk to your stepmother about this some more?" He sipped his soda.

She took a drink of water. "I guess I should. Mom's hiding something. I can feel it." She looked at him, trying hard not to stare into his gorgeous brown eyes.

He sighed, looking sullen. "Like I said earlier, it looks as if your dad *may* have been planning to sell, but I can't tell for sure."

She gripped her water glass. "You're kidding," she mumbled.

"Sweetheart, I wouldn't joke about something like this."

The endearment rolled off his tongue and settled into her heart. She ignored the feeling, again focusing on the news he'd delivered. "Well, you're wrong. My dad would not sell the farm. I've never met a person who loved dairy farming more than Paul Cooper. Plus, my dad inherited our farm from his father. My grandfather was one of the first African-American dairy farmers in Baltimore County. Dairy farming is in our blood, and I can't imagine my father giving that up."

He gazed at her with his warm, dark eyes. "You're probably right. You seem to know your dad pretty well. He may have been contacting a Realtor for a different reason."

A horrible thought occurred to her. "Do you think my stepmother wants to sell, and she just hasn't told me?" The thought sickened her. When her plate of jambalaya arrived, Emily pushed it away, her appetite gone.

Frank massaged her fingers. "Are you sure you're okay?"

She didn't answer his question, finding comfort in his touch. Reluctantly she pulled her hand away.

"You didn't answer my question, Frank."

He sampled his shrimp before responding. "Emily, I honestly don't know. Maybe you should call your stepmom tonight and try and talk to her about all of this."

"Yeah, I just might do that." She stared at her food, suddenly wanting to go home and place the call in private. Frank continued to eat, and Emily prayed before she sampled her meal. When they finished, Emily requested a take-out box for her leftovers.

Afterward they walked around Harborplace before they returned to Frank's car. He drove her home and cut off the ignition when they arrived at her farm. "Do you mind if we sit on your porch?"

The thought of sitting with Frank on the porch on a star-filled night made her feel warm and cozy. "No, I don't mind at all." They walked to the porch and sat on the swing.

As they gently swayed, Frank spoke. "Are you sure you're okay?"

She nodded. "I'm okay. I just don't know what kinds of things my stepmother is hiding." She looked at him. "I also don't like what you told me about my dad. I feel like I'm being lied to."

He sighed. "Emily. . ."

She shook her head. "I guess you'll be back next week to continue working in my dad's office?"

"Yes, I'll be back next week. I'm not sure what time, though, because I have some meetings to attend." Crickets chirped in the hot summer air. Emily's stomach flipped when Frank held her hand. Sparks of warmth shot up her arm, and she couldn't gather the courage to pull her hand away. "Can I ask you something?"

She looked at him. "What?"

"I really had a good time tonight. I also enjoyed having dinner with you when we went to Michael's Pizza."

She smiled, her belly curling with warmth. "Yeah, I had a good time, too."

"I wondered if you wanted to get together again sometime next week. Maybe we can go to a movie or something." He squeezed her hand. "I like spending time with you, and I want to get to know you better."

She pulled her hand away. "I'll be honest with you. I like spending time with you, too, but there are things about you that bother me."

"What kinds of things?"

"Well, for starters, when we went to Michael's Pizza, I noticed the liquor bottles in your car."

He grunted. "I saw you frown when you saw the alcohol, but I didn't give it much thought."

The swing rocked as she gathered her thoughts. "Do you drink every day?"

"Yes."

"Why? When did you start doing this?"

He threw his hands up in the air, frowning. "Why is it such a big deal? Why are you asking me these questions?"

"You just asked about us going out. These are things I need to know about somebody before I agree to a date."

He sighed. "When something heavy is on my mind, I drink to forget. I've been doing this for about a year now. I've had problems with it before that, but I was able to quit eventually."

"What's on your mind?"

"It's kind of complicated. My parents did some awful things, and I can't let my anger go."

"Frank, you really need to forgive your parents for what they've done. If their actions are causing you to drink, then you need to do something else to deal with your pain."

"I'm almost afraid to ask what you would do if you were me."

"Are you a Christian?"

"I believe in God."

She shook her head, looking at him. "I didn't ask if you believed in God. I asked if you're a Christian."

"I've noticed that a lot of people say they are Christians, but it doesn't necessarily mean the same thing to everybody."

She sensed he was avoiding her question, so she decided to be more direct. "When I use the term *Christian*, I'm referring to somebody who has accepted Christ as their Savior and who trusts Him completely. Can you honestly tell me you've done this?"

When he remained silent, she continued. "Do you go to church regularly?"

"No, I don't."

"Do you consider yourself to be a Christian?"

He hesitated before responding. "Not really."

She looked away, stunned upon hearing this news. Her attraction to Frank was deep, deeper than she imagined possible given the circumstances. She loved spending time with him and wished something could develop between them. However, she knew even if this was what she wanted, she had to follow the Lord's Word and not get involved with a non-Christian. She clenched her hands together, taking a deep breath before speaking. "I don't think it's a good idea for us to spend time together socially anymore."

"Why?" Exasperation tinged his voice.

"If I'm going to spend time with somebody, I want to make sure he's a Christian. My belief in God is the one thing that's constant and keeps me centered in this crazy world."

"We can still date and get to know each other better. You can't deny that we're attracted to each other."

Their attraction was so strong that it was a bit scary. Emily didn't know what she'd do with herself if she continued to see Frank and then fall for him. "Have you thought about getting help for your problem?"

"What problem?"

"Your heavy drinking problem. There's an alcoholic support group at my church—"

"I'm not an alcoholic."

"You don't get drunk?" He didn't respond. "Your eyes were red this morning, and you said you didn't feel well. Were you sick, or were you hungover?"

His lips settled into a grim line, and he stared out into the cornfield. Another concern struck her. "Do you ever drive after you drink?"

He shook his head. "No. I only drink after I get home for the night." She was surprised when he abruptly changed the subject. "Are you seeing anybody right now?"

"No."

"When was the last time you were in a serious relationship?"

She knitted her brow. "Why are you asking me this?"

He shrugged. "I'm just curious. I like you, and I want to know more about you."

She sighed, not wanting to talk about Jamal, but decided to humor Frank's curiosity. "I was engaged once."

His long-lashed eyes widened, and he encouraged her to continue.

"I met Jamal in grad school."

"You went to grad school?"

She nodded. "I have a master's degree in agriculture. Both Jamal and I graduated a little over a year ago from the University of Maryland."

"Well, what happened? Why aren't the two of you married?"

"I thought we both wanted the same things. I felt he made some wrong assumptions about me, and he just couldn't accept me for the way I was."

He gazed at the cornfield in the distance. "What kind of assumptions did he make?"

The negative memories washed over her. "Well, for starters, he didn't know I wanted to continue farming."

"Whoa. I've only known you for a few days, and even I can see how much you love farming. What were you all going to do?"

She gave him a puzzled look. "What do you mean?"

"Well, did you expect him to move into the house with you and your parents?"

She shook her head. "No, nothing like that. Since I thought we were planning to stay in the Baltimore County area, I was going to continue working for my dad. I'd planned on commuting to the farm from our new home."

"I still don't understand what the problem was. Besides, you were getting your degree in agriculture. Isn't that a clue that you'd want to stay in the farming business?"

Emily chuckled, recalling her aborted engagement. "Well, sometimes Jamal was pretty clueless."

"What did he want you to do?"

"He found a good job with an engineering firm, but it was located in Texas, so we'd have to move. He said once we were married and settled into our new lives in Texas, he didn't want me to work."

"What?"

Emily nodded. "He wanted me to be a stay-at-home wife and have kids and be a family woman." She shrugged. "Again, I just assumed he knew what I wanted. I would love to have my own family, but I wanted to be a farmer, too. Since he wanted me to give up my profession, he obviously didn't know me very well."

"Is that the only reason you broke up?"

"Isn't that enough?"

He shrugged. "I guess, but I was wondering if anything else happened between you two."

She continued to think about her former fiancé. "Well, he

said he was a Christian, and I thought he loved the Lord like I did."

He frowned. "What made you think that he didn't love God?"

She gathered her thoughts. "We were attracted to each other. We were *very* attracted to each other. When our engagement was official, he started pressuring me to make love to him. I told him I wanted to wait until after we were married, but he wouldn't let it go. We argued about it constantly, and we also argued about my continuing to farm after the wedding." She frowned. "It got to the point where I dreaded his phone calls and visits until I finally gave him his ring back. I started to feel like a prop."

"A prop?"

She nodded. "Yeah. I felt like an actress or something."

"I don't know what you mean."

"Well, after I met him, we didn't date for very long before we were engaged. Everything was so rushed that I felt like we didn't get to know each other very much. I sensed he was desperate to get married and have a family, and I was there, dating him. We were attracted, so he asked me to marry him." She sighed. "I don't think we were really in love. I felt like an actress, playing the role of his fiancée, without his knowing me as a person."

A warm breeze blew, tickling her cheek. When Frank took her hand, the warmth enveloped her fingers. "If you felt that way, why did you get engaged?"

"Initially I wasn't honest with myself. I made excuses for our arguments and his behavior. Soon I got tired of making excuses, and I was just honest with myself. I sensed the Lord was telling me that Jamal wasn't the right man to spend my life with."

She mentally sighed when Frank seemed to be content with her answer. They silently rocked in the swing, holding hands, his leg jiggling.

Headlights of a car turning into her driveway shined on them, and Frank dropped her hand. Kelly and Christine soon strolled toward the porch.

Frank frowned, staring at the women. "Who are they?"

five

Emily touched Frank's arm. "That's Kelly and Christine, my friends."

Kelly clutched a white grocery bag, and Christine held a box of Cinnabon rolls. "Hi," Kelly greeted. "Christine and I didn't realize you'd have company tonight," she said, looking at Frank.

Emily gestured toward Frank. "He's not company. This is Franklin Reese; he's our new accountant."

Kelly raised one perfectly arched eyebrow, and Emily sensed she was assessing Frank's physical attributes. She stuck out her hand. "Nice to meet you. I'm Kelly, and this is Christine."

Once Kelly shook Frank's hand, Christine did the same. "Hi, ladies."

She looked at Frank before gesturing toward the house. "I guess I'll see you on Monday?"

Frank stood, causing the swing to rock. "Yes, I'll be here on Monday." He exited the porch and waved to the women before he got into his car and drove away.

Kelly placed her hands on her hips, and Christine stood behind her. "He stood me up! This is the last time I accept a date with that loser!" said Kelly.

They stepped into the house, and Emily turned on the kitchen light. She saw how much time Kelly had taken to prepare for her date. Her black hair was swept into an elegant bun, and she wore a new pantsuit. Expensive perfume wafted through the room as Kelly tossed her grocery sack on the scarred kitchen table and Christine placed the Cinnabon box beside it. Kelly pulled out two small ice cream cartons. "I got

53

ice cream for both of us."

Christine pointed to her treat. "And I brought cinnamon rolls for myself." She rolled her eyes at Kelly. "She had the nerve to interrupt my lazy Saturday night." She gazed at Emily. "I was going to spend this evening lounging around in my silk pajamas and reading a book and eating my cinnamon rolls with a cup of coffee." She looked at Kelly. "Then she appeared on my doorstep, distraught that Martin had stood her up, and she insisted we come to visit you so both of us could cheer her up in person. She stopped for ice cream on the way."

Emily sat, placing her head in her hand. "I'm not hungry now. I'm glad you brought me ice cream, but I can't eat another bite." She pointed to her take-out container. "Frank and I ate at the Cheesecake Factory."

Kelly popped the ice cream carton open and fished a spoon from a drawer. "The Cheesecake Factory?" She sat, giving Emily a hard look. "Since when do you go out to The Cheesecake Factory with your business associates?" She grabbed Emily's arm. "I thought you said Frank wouldn't be a good prospect because of his drinking."

Christine sat beside Kelly, taking a bite of her roll before speaking. "His drinking?"

Emily explained that she saw liquor bottles in Frank's car. "We were talking about his drinking earlier tonight."

Christine spoke. "Oh, I'm sorry, Emily. If we'd known, we wouldn't have stopped by."

"I'm glad you guys came by. Frank didn't want to talk about it anyway."

"He wouldn't talk about his drinking problem?"

Emily shook her head. "He got upset when I asked him about it. I feel like he's denying he has a problem."

"What kind of problems could he be having that would cause him to drink so much?" asked Christine.

"I'm not sure. He mentioned that it had to do with his parents, but he didn't give many details."

"Do you mind if I make myself some coffee to go with my rolls?" asked Christine.

Emily stood, wanting to do something busy. "I'll do it." Fresh coffee soon dripped into the pot. When it was finished perking, she asked Kelly if she wanted some coffee, but she declined, so Emily poured two cups and removed the milk from the refrigerator and carried it to the table. She placed the sugar container beside the milk, and Emily and Christine sipped their coffee.

Kelly placed a large chunk of ice cream into her mouth. "Mmm. This is the best remedy for a broken heart."

Emily scoffed. "You only went out with Martin once. You haven't even known him long enough to have a broken heart!"

Kelly rolled her eyes, sampling another bite of ice cream. "Whatever. I thought he had great potential."

"After only one date?" Christine interjected.

"But last week's date was great!" She dropped her spoon on the table and modeled her recently manicured nails. "See, I even got my nails done." The red, oval-shaped nails matched her outfit, and Emily could hear Kelly's disappointment. "I've wasted my whole day getting ready for Martin, only to be disappointed."

"Did you call him?" Emily asked.

Kelly raised her eyebrows, scowling at Emily. "Of course not. If I call him, he'll see how anxious I am."

Christine spoke. "Maybe you should call him anyway. Something might have happened. What if he was in an accident or something?"

Kelly widened her eyes. "Do you think something could have happened to him?"

"It's hard to say," Emily said. "Why don't you call him, and if he doesn't answer, you could leave him a message."

Kelly pulled her cell phone out of her purse and pressed a few buttons. She spoke into the receiver, leaving Martin a message. She snapped her phone shut. "Hopefully he'll call me back tonight or tomorrow."

Christine spoke. "I wanted you all to see my new purse."

Emily fingered the expensive handbag, and Kelly rolled her eyes. "You know you can't afford that, Christine. If you want my advice—"

"Which I don't."

Kelly pursed her lips. "Whatever. But don't come crying to me to borrow money when you can't pay your bills. If you want to do what's good for you, you'd take that purse back to the store tomorrow."

Emily had learned a long time ago that you couldn't reason with Christine. She decided to tell them about the discussion she'd had earlier with Frank. "You'll never believe what Frank told me tonight." She glanced at the clock. "I wanted to call Mom and talk to her about it, but I'm sure she's in bed now." She told them what Frank said about the files he'd found on her father's computer, implying he may have been planning to sell their farm shortly before his death.

"Whoa!" Kelly interjected. "That's deep. Do you think your stepmom knew about this?"

Emily shrugged. "I don't know. I sense she might be trying to protect me from something. . . ." She thought about it for a few minutes. "It makes my head spin when I think about it too much. My father is the last person who would sell this place. He always said he would farm until he died." She covered her lips when tears came to her eyes. "And he did farm until he died." Her mouth quivered, and she went to the sink and got a glass of water. A few tears spilled onto her cheeks, and Kelly and Christine were beside her in seconds, hugging her. "I miss Daddy so much, guys. It hurts so bad."

Christine squeezed her friend's shoulder. "I wish there was

something I could do for you. With the Lord's help, it won't hurt so much after a while." Emily breathed deeply and wiped her eyes. Kelly handed her tissues, and Emily dried her eyes and drank her water.

"There's nothing anybody can do to make me feel better." They returned to the table as she continued to speak. "You know, I feel like such a loser."

"Why?" asked Kelly.

"I loved my dad and I miss him, but I seem to be the only one in my family who's taking his death so hard." She gestured toward the phone. "When I talk to Laura, she sounds happier than she was here at the farm. It almost makes me wonder if she's planning on never coming back."

Kelly slapped Emily's arm. "Stop saying such nonsense. She'll come home. I'm sure a change of scenery is helping her deal with her grief. What about your sister?"

"You know I only hear from Sarah when she needs something. Since she doesn't live nearby, it's not like I can just drop by her house and commiserate about Dad."

Christine sighed. "Emily, you can always call your sister. I'm sure she'd find the time to talk to you. Besides, you don't know how Sarah is dealing with your father's death."

Emily shook her head before changing the subject. "You know, I was cleaning up earlier, and I found a stack of programs from my dad's funeral service. Remember my cousin Monica?"

Christine nodded. "Yeah, she's the woman who just got married a year ago and lives on the Eastern shore. I remember she's older than we are. One summer when she was staying at your farm, she drove all three of us to Baltimore to go to the movies."

"Well, remember she was at the funeral with her new husband?"

Kelly nodded.

"She scribbled her new phone number on one of the

programs and told me to call her if I needed anything."

Kelly shrugged. "Have you called her?"

"No, I figured she wouldn't want to hear from me."

"Why?" asked Christine.

"You know how people are at funerals. They always say call me if you need anything, and half the time they don't really mean it."

Kelly snorted. "And half the time they do. You should call your cousin."

"I still might give her a call to talk. She used to like visiting here when she was younger. Maybe I can invite her and her new husband to come over sometime."

"That sounds like a good idea. You can give her a call in the meantime," commented Kelly, scraping the last of the ice cream from the container. Once she ate the last bite, she smiled warmly.

"I can't believe you ate that whole carton of ice cream," said Emily.

Kelly nodded. "I did, and now I feel so much better."

A cow bellowed from the barn. "Frank and I went to the auction today; then we went to dinner afterward because we were hungry." Since Christine didn't know, Emily explained how Frank had helped her with a breach birth.

"Maybe you can invite him to church and try to convert him," suggested Christine.

"Convert him?"

"Yeah, invite him to church and share the gospel with him. Maybe he's bitter about something and mad at God."

"Do you really think I should ask him to visit our church?"

"Yeah, of course. What do you think God would want you to do?" asked Christine.

Emily silently thought about Kelly's and Christine's advice.

Kelly patted her full stomach. "Isn't it a shame? Another good-looking man wasted? All three of us are twenty-eight, and it looks like we'll never find husbands." She gazed at Emily. "Do you remember what you used to tell me when we were teenagers? You used to daydream about your ideal husband."

Emily grinned, recalling those times. "Yes, I used to say that my husband would be living on the farm with me, and we'd be working side by side, taking care of the cows, raising kids together."

Kelly continued. "Well, I'm wondering if any of us is ever going to find a husband. You haven't been serious about anybody since you broke up with Jamal a year ago. You haven't even been on a date since."

Before Kelly and Christine took their exit, the three women joined hands and prayed for one another.

❧

Frank pulled into the liquor store parking lot. He sat in the car for a few minutes, digesting all that had happened that day. He'd struggled all day and all evening about asking Emily out on a date. He was attracted to her, and even though he was upset with her decision about not spending time with him, he couldn't really blame her for her choice. He respected that she stuck with her beliefs, and he felt he needed to make more of an effort to put her out of his mind. When they were sitting on her porch, he had suddenly realized this was the first day in a long time that he hadn't thought about Julie. It was that thought that had bolstered him to ask her on a date.

Her refusal of his invitation was probably for the best. They were definitely not suited for one another. He exited his car, and his cell phone vibrated in his pocket as he entered the establishment. He flipped his phone open and walked toward the shelf that displayed his favorite scotch. "What do you want, Trish?" The sound of his sister crying made him stop. He softened his voice. "What's wrong?"

"Frank, it's Mark."

His heart skipped a beat. "Did he get hurt?" he asked hurriedly.

She sniffed. "No, nothing like that." In a tearful voice, she told her brother that Mark had met some friends that day to go to the movies. Afterward they went to a store nearby, and they were caught shoplifting. "The security guard called me, and I had to go get him." She continued to cry. "Frank, I don't know what to do with my son. He's been so angry since his father left."

"Did you want me to talk to him?"

"No, he's in bed now." She paused for a few seconds. "I wanted to ask if you can come down one weekend soon and spend some time with Mark. His father was supposed to come and visit the last two weekends, but he didn't show up. Mark's gotten worse since his father has stood him up." She choked on a sob. "I'll understand if you can't come."

"No, let me check my workload, and I'll see if I can come down sometime soon." He rang off with his sister as he lifted the bottle of scotch from the shelf.

❧

A few days later the screen door banged shut when Emily entered the house. Minutes passed and Frank figured she was changing out of her barn boots before she entered her home. He noted the late hour before she peeked into the room.

He looked up, adjusting his glasses, when she entered. Tendrils of hair spilled from her ponytail, giving her an earthy, mussed appearance. "Frank, it's almost nine o'clock."

He blinked, pulled his glasses off, and rubbed his eyes. "I know. Why are you just now coming in from the barn?"

Sighing, she sat in a chair. "One of the cows was sick. I was just making sure she was okay. I think I'll call the vet tomorrow." She glanced around the office. "Why are you still here?"

"I'm missing some of your father's files."

She frowned. "What are you missing?"

He explained which financial papers he was looking for. "I'm going to have trouble finishing my audit if I don't find those papers."

"Well, I'm sure they're around here someplace." She stood and pulled out a drawer in one of the filing cabinets. "Have you looked in here?"

He nodded. "There's a few filing cabinets in the other corner that are locked. I didn't know where the key was."

Emily lifted a bright yellow mug from the desk and dumped the contents. Frank helped her sift through the mess, and his fingers brushed against hers. Warmth traveled over his hand. She spotted the key. "Here it is."

She rushed to the cabinet, placing the key into the hole. A soft click sounded as she unlocked the drawer. She pulled, but it failed to open. "Frank, I think it's stuck," she gasped, still trying to open the drawer.

He rushed to her side. Together they opened the drawer, and folders tumbled onto the floor. He whistled softly, gazing at the papers. "Your father sure does keep a lot of stuff around."

Nodding, she massaged her neck, and he wondered if she was tired from a long day of work. "I hardly spent any time in this office. I don't really know what's in here." Pulling out one of the folders, she flipped it open, finding notes written in pencil. "This makes no sense to me. It's just a bunch of numbers."

He glanced at the notes and frowned. "Well, whatever this is, it's not what we're looking for." He glanced at the cabinet again. "But we might need to go through this whole cabinet to find the papers we need."

"Maybe we should do this another time. I don't feel like looking through this stuff right now. It's late."

Changing the subject, he pulled a family photograph off her father's desk. "Is this your stepmother and your sister?"

She nodded, glancing at the picture. Emily looked like she was about eighteen in the photo. "Yes, I think I was telling you about my sister when we had dinner at the pizza place."

He sat, still looking at the photo. "Why do you look so upset in this picture?"

"Because my father had just gotten remarried, and I was not eager to have a new female in this house. That picture was taken right before my sister, Sarah, left home. That's why you see her smiling. She was getting ready to leave the farm, and she was relieved because she always hated it."

"Were you angry that your sister left?"

She shrugged, glancing around the cluttered office. "It worked out okay. I love it here, and I don't mind being the only sister left behind to take care of the family business."

"Do you talk to your sister often?"

"Not really."

"Do the two of you get along?"

"It depends. Sometimes we do, and sometimes we don't. She only calls me when she wants to borrow money."

"Really?"

She nodded.

"Does she usually pay you back?"

"Sometimes she does. We were never really close even though we lived in the same house. My daddy used to say we were like oil and water."

"What happened to your real mother?"

"She died of breast cancer when I was fifteen. Things were pretty rough out here on the farm when she passed."

"Things were rough because you were grieving?"

"Sort of. Remember, I told you Sarah hated farming?"

He nodded.

"Well, when Mom died, she refused to do anything. She wouldn't help out with the chores. She'd yell at my dad; she called me names." She shook her head, looking away. "My dad had to ask our church if they knew about any type of counseling services he could use for Sarah."

He stared at her, wanting to take her into his arms and tell her he was sorry that she'd now lost both of her parents. Instead, he asked another question. "How did you deal with your grief when your mother died? It's obvious that your sister turned rebellious."

"I spent most of my time in the barn or in the field with the cows, alone." She folded her arms in front of her. "It was awful. It took me a long time to get over losing my mom."

"Sarah's reaction reminds me of what my sister is going through now."

"What do you mean?"

"Remember I told you about her husband leaving?"

"Yes, I remember."

He told her about Trish's recent phone call and Mark's rebellious behavior. "I have to find some time soon to go and see Mark. I miss him, and I want to do everything I can to make him feel better."

"I'm sorry your nephew is hurting so much."

"I'm sure my sister's life would have been a lot better if she'd never married that guy."

"Frank, you don't know that."

He gritted his teeth. "I never trusted him, and I tried to warn her, but she wouldn't listen to me. Every boy needs a good, stable father at home, and it makes me mad that Mark and Regina's dad doesn't even seem to care."

"You really feel strongly about this, don't you?"

"Yes, it makes me upset when so many young boys are out there and they don't have fathers to turn to." He told her about the rec center in Chicago and the youth he used to mentor.

Her dark eyes widened. "You used to mentor youth?"

He nodded.

"Have you done this since you've been in Maryland?"

He shook his head, almost sorry he'd said as much as he had. He didn't feel like going into the reasons why he'd stopped mentoring one year ago.

Emily frowned as she looked away.

"What's the matter?" he asked.

"Nothing. I was just thinking about something."

He looked at the bulging pile of paper, no longer wanting to talk about his sister and his activities in Chicago. "We have tons of stuff to go through. I hope we can find everything I need."

"How is the audit coming along so far? I'm sure my father's financial records are in good order."

"I can't comment until I'm finished. Do you understand everything we've been going through together? Are you having any problems with the financial software I showed you how to use?"

She frowned. "I think I understand, sort of." She gestured around the office. "I'm still not used to handling all this. It's a lot of information for me to remember."

"Either myself or somebody in the firm can always advise you about financial matters."

"People are always telling me and Laura that we should have gotten more involved in the finances of our farm, and I'm starting to see they were right." She gave Frank a small smile. "But I'm just concerned about figuring out how this farm is doing and making sure we can continue the routine you've taught me during the last few days for our bookkeeping."

"Well, I still have to start a few audits at some other farms, and I'm at a standstill with your audit." He opened his briefcase and removed a business card. He flipped it over, writing his information on the back. "I'm leaving my business card. My work number is on the front, and I'm writing my home number on the back. My e-mail address is listed there, too." He pressed the card into her hand, relishing the warmth of her skin. He hesitated before pulling his hand away, still trying hard to ignore their attraction.

He sat at the computer and opened a document, his leg jiggling. "Even though we've been through the whole budgeting and bookkeeping process together, I've still typed up notes for you and your stepmom about the accounting process for your farm. I tried to make the file easy for you to use." He pressed a few keys on the keyboard. "Laura might need my detailed notes since she wasn't here when I was teaching you everything."

"So you're all finished?" He wished he could keep coming here each day, but being around Emily was torturous, knowing how she felt about his personal life and beliefs.

He told her the truth. "No, not completely. I have some loose ends to tie up, but I can do those at the office. Remember those papers I was telling you about?"

"Yes?"

"Well, when you find those, I can complete the audit." He glanced at the papers piled on the floor. "I don't want to waste time searching for something since we charge by the hour." He pulled a notebook from his briefcase. "I'm going to write down what I'm looking for." He scribbled the information, sensing Emily watching him the entire time. When he was finished, he pointed to the last two items. "I can't find your father's tax returns for the last couple of years."

Her mouth dropped open. "I know he filed his taxes—"

He touched her arm, and she calmed down. "I know he did. When I was going through his bank statements, I could see the direct deposits in his account from the IRS tax refund. But it'll still help me out if I could find those files." He glanced around the office again. "I know they're around here someplace."

"You want me to look for the things you have listed here?"

He nodded. "Please. When you find them, I can come back

out here and complete my job, or, if you prefer that I not come, you can scan and e-mail the files to my office."

Silence surrounded them, and Frank was at a loss for words. Since she'd had her conversation with him about his drinking and her religious beliefs, they'd continued working together in her father's office, sometimes making small talk. The attraction he felt for her refused to go away, so maybe it was best that he not return to her home after all. She finally spoke. "I can probably scan them and e-mail them to you if it's quicker. I don't want to waste your time by making you come out here." She tucked his card into her pocket and sat in the chair beside the filing cabinet, stacking the manila folders into a pile.

Frank stood beside the computer, and his heart pitter-pattered. "It's never a waste of time coming out here." The urge to kiss her rushed through him, but Julie's face hovered on the fringes of his mind. Emily dumped some folders into a box, mumbling about looking through them later. She picked up the container and walked into the kitchen, and Frank followed her, holding his briefcase and car keys. He wondered when he'd see her again. She placed the box on the table and walked him to the door. He stood on the porch and stared at Emily. Before he could stop himself, his lips brushed hers. She backed away, her pretty eyes widening.

"I didn't mean for that to happen," he mumbled. Crickets chirped, and the scent of animals and hay wafted around them. Her mesmerizing eyes were beautiful when she looked at him. He stepped back into the kitchen and closed the door, not wanting to leave anything unsaid between them.

"I'm sorry for kissing you," he said. "I hope you're not upset."

"Your lack of faith in God bothers me, Frank. Your drinking bothers me, too." She walked to the window, gazing at the barn.

"I know." She glanced at him, her sullen expression making

his heart ache. "My drinking's been bothering me lately, too." Lately he'd been drinking more alcohol at night to get a buzz, and Trish was still calling him all the time, telling him he needed to get help.

She remained by the window, still looking at him. "Have you had a drink today?"

He shook his head. "No, not yet. That's why I'm still here. I didn't have a chance to tell you the other day that if I work late so my mind is tired, I may not drink as much when I go home." He clutched the handle of his briefcase. "But usually the memories and the nightmares bother me no matter what I do." The drinking always calmed him, soothed him, making it possible for him to fall asleep, even though there was sometimes a price to pay the following day. Since he'd started drinking more, he'd woken up sick to his stomach more often.

"You're haunted by something. What is it?" Her sweet voice softened.

"Nothing I want to talk about right now."

"There's an alcoholic support group at my church—"

He held up his hand. "I don't want to go."

"But it might help you," she pleaded. "You know, your lack of faith in God bothers me even more than your drinking." She turned toward the window again. "Maybe it's best that you've finished most of the audit for us."

The rusty hinges on the door squeaked as he opened it. "I'll e-mail you and your mother a report about what I've done so far. Just let me know when you've found those documents."

The screen door banged shut when he left, and he noticed Emily still standing in the window, watching him as he pulled out of her driveway.

six

The next day Emily awakened earlier than usual. She spent a leisurely hour reading a few psalms, finding comfort in the lyrical words. Both Jeremy and Darren arrived to help with the milking. After lunch the boys' father arrived plus a few other people she'd hired to help with the three-day chore of making hay.

The day bustled with activity, and Emily was glad for the extra physical exercise. She hoped that if she was tired enough by the end of the day, Frank wouldn't dominate her thoughts. During the day Emily found herself daydreaming about his kiss. She again wished he'd listen to her and take her advice about accepting Christ in addition to getting help for his drinking. She also found herself thinking about the role he was playing in his sister's life with her kids and about the fact that he used to mentor youth while living in Chicago. She wondered if Frank wanted to have children someday, but she pushed those thoughts from her mind, not wanting to dwell on that subject too much.

Fatigue settled in Emily's bones after Jeremy and Darren had helped her with the evening milking. She enjoyed a sub for supper then took a quick shower and changed before trudging to her truck. The repairman at the shop had stressed that she might want to start looking for a new vehicle. "This one is on its last leg and I don't know how much longer we're going to be able to repair it," he'd said.

She sipped from the thermos of coffee, thinking about the repairman's advice. She knew she would probably have to look for a used truck. She'd already called Laura, telling her what the repair shop had said about the truck and about what Frank had told her the previous day.

"Frank already called and told me everything," her step-mother had said.

"He did?" Emily didn't know why she was so surprised. Frank had mentioned that he needed to talk to her mother since Laura was the one who had requested the services of their firm.

"I can tell that something is heavy on your mind," her mother had said. "Did the accountant explain everything to you?"

"Yes, he explained everything in detail. Mom, when are you coming home? I miss you."

"I miss you, too. I promise I'll be home soon."

She continued to drive, putting the whole conversation out of her mind. She pulled into the parking lot of Monkton Christian Church for her volunteer committee meeting. During the meeting, she could barely keep her eyes open. Christine and Kelly were present, and when it was over, the three friends exited the building together. "Girl, you sure do look tired," Kelly said to Emily. "You're going to run yourself ragged working on that farm."

Emily mentioned they'd cut the alfalfa that day with the haybine. "Once it dries out over the next day or so, we're going to have to bale it."

"Sounds like a lot of work."

Emily nodded. "It is. I'm so tired."

Christine touched Emily's arm. "During the committee meeting, you looked like you had something on your mind."

"I do."

"What's the matter? Has Laura said something to upset you?" asked Kelly as they walked into the parking lot.

"No, I miss Laura like crazy, but that's not why I'm upset."

"Well, what's wrong?" Christine demanded. Their cars were

parked side by side, and they stood in front of their vehicles. Emily debated about telling them what happened the previous evening.

"Why don't we go and get a snack at the Wagon Wheel?" suggested Kelly.

"I'll go, but I'm not staying a long time," said Emily.

They were soon seated at the restaurant. After purchasing slices of cake and cups of coffee and tea, they sat at a table in the back. Emily sipped her drink before telling her news. "Frank kissed me last night."

Kelly's mouth dropped open. "Whoa. You're kidding!"

"Are you serious?" asked Christine.

Emily nodded. "Yes, I wasn't expecting it."

Kelly stirred her coffee. "Are you going to see him again?"

Emily shook her head. "No, not unless I have to talk to him about the audit. I don't think it's a good idea for me to see him again. Once I find the documents he's looking for, I'll scan them and e-mail them to him. Once he's finished, I won't have to see him again."

"How long do you think it will take you to forget about Frank?" Christine asked.

"I'm not sure. This is awful, but I miss him already. I know there's no hope for us since he's not even a Christian."

"There still might be hope for you and Frank," Kelly said. "Leave everything in the Lord's hands and see what happens."

"Thanks, Kelly." She glanced at her other friend. "Christine, I notice you're wearing a nice pair of diamond earrings. Were they a gift?"

Kelly sipped her drink. "What do you think, Em? Do you really think it was a gift? You know she probably charged her earrings."

Christine touched her earlobes, frowning. "I got these on sale at a new jewelry store that opened at Harborplace. I couldn't resist since they were such a good price."

"Has anything else been going on with you, Christine?" asked Emily.

Christine placed her chin in her hand, gazing at her friends. "I do have a confession to make."

"What's that?" asked Kelly.

"I purchased these earrings for a reason."

"And what reason might that be?" asked Kelly.

"They had a meeting at work today. Some of us are going to be laid off within the next few months."

"Christine, I'm sorry," Emily said, touching her hand. "I know how much you like working there."

"So you purchased the earrings because you were upset about the imminent layoff?" asked Kelly, furrowing her brow.

Emily moved to touch Kelly's hand, knowing how upset Kelly became whenever Christine went on a shopping binge. "I think she's trying to tell us that she purchased the earrings because they made her feel better."

"Whatever," said Kelly, rolling her eyes. "You shouldn't be using material things to make yourself feel better, Christine. You said you might be out of a job soon, so buying a pair of diamond earrings won't make things better."

Christine shrugged. "I know they won't make things better, but they make me feel better. Do you understand?"

Kelly shrugged. "I guess."

Emily spoke to Kelly. "You're awfully quiet about what's been happening in your life lately. Have you heard from Martin?"

"Yes," Kelly responded.

Emily and Christine looked at Kelly expectantly. "Well?" asked Emily. "What did he say?"

"He said he forgot about our date the other night."

Christine asked, "Well, did he at least offer to take you out again?"

"No," Kelly responded.

"How come?" asked Emily.

Kelly's mouth was set in a grim line. "You guys, no offense, but this is not something I'm ready to talk about right now."

Emily hugged her friend. "We don't mean to pry. If something's bothering you, then you know you can talk to me and Christine about it." Christine nodded, her dark eyes full of sympathy.

When they were finished with their snacks, Emily hugged her friends before she drove home. Once she'd read her Bible, she crawled into bed and said a brief prayer before she fell asleep.

seven

The days passed, and Emily still couldn't put Frank out of her mind. She thought about him daily, even though he no longer came to her house. Memories of his kiss lingered, and she prayed, waiting for the feelings to disappear.

During the July Fourth holiday, she rode to Baltimore's Inner Harbor with Christine and Kelly to see the fireworks. Bursts of color exploded in the dark sky, illuminating the pedestrians and couples strolling the sidewalks. Longing pierced her when she observed couple after couple holding hands or nestling in each other's arms to watch the fireworks.

A few days following the July Fourth fireworks, Emily was thinking about the last time she'd seen Frank when she pulled into a parking space on Pratt Street, across from the Inner Harbor. She opened her purse, searching for coins to feed the meter. After the annual evening meeting with the Maryland farmers' association, she felt like taking some time and walking along the Inner Harbor alone. It was a blessing that both Jeremy and Darren came to milk the cows earlier, giving her the freedom to attend the event. She checked her watch, noting it was eight o'clock. She still had some time to stroll around before the shops closed.

She continued searching for change, thinking about Laura. She missed her like crazy, and the loneliness on the farm was eating away at her. When she'd spoken to her a few days ago, she'd told her about the papers missing from her father's office and that she was searching for the paperwork Frank needed to continue his audit. She'd already found and e-mailed him a few of the files, but the rest of the documents were still missing. When she'd asked Laura about her father selling the farm, she'd claimed it was hard to know for sure what her father had planned on doing.

She gasped when Frank exited the upscale liquor store located on the waterfront of the Inner Harbor. He clutched a large paper sack, and Emily was again reminded about how different their beliefs were and how their attraction seemed to escalate, in spite of their unshared faith. His head was down as he hurried toward his car, and Emily couldn't resist calling out his name. She rolled down her window and yelled. "Frank!" He stopped and looked toward her, his dark eyes appearing startled. He clutched his paper bag and strolled toward her truck.

"Emily, what are you doing here?"

She inhaled the familiar scent of his cologne as she looked at him. "I was at a local farmer's association meeting downtown. I just came over here to take a walk."

He remained silent, and she glanced at the bag. Sweat beaded his brow, so he wiped it away. "I had to pick something up before going back to my apartment."

"Oh." She suddenly felt nervous.

Frank relaxed against her truck. "It's hot out here. Did you want to come up to my apartment and cool off for a bit? I only live a few blocks away. We could share a few drinks."

She eyed the paper bag. "I don't think so."

"Emily, I was going to give you some lemonade. I made it myself. You don't have to stay long. I have some things concerning the audit that I was going to talk to you about."

She swallowed, noting her throat was very parched. A cold glass of lemonade did sound good, so she started the ignition. "Just lead the way."

Once he'd gotten in his car, she followed him to his apartment building. A basketball court was outside, and a group of young people played a game in the intense summer heat. A few of the boys spotted Frank, calling out his name. "Hey, Mr. Frank, you want to shoot some hoops with us?"

He waved. "Maybe tomorrow."

As they rode the elevator, Emily spoke. "You play basketball with them often?"

"No, not too often." They soon entered his cool loft apartment. "Sorry it's such a mess." He picked up a few clothes and threw them into the corner. Take-out Chinese and pizza boxes littered the area, and she assumed Frank hated cooking. She could certainly understand, because she'd been living off sandwiches and fast food ever since Laura left for Florida.

She felt the place could be charming and cozy with a woman's touch and a few decorations. The kitchen was spotless, and she supposed he barely used that room. "How is your nephew doing?"

He lifted a pair of shoes and placed them in the hall closet. "He's doing a little bit better. He recently had a birthday, and I was able to go to Chicago for the weekend for his party."

She smiled, enjoying the grin that split Frank's handsome face as he spoke of his nephew. "I'm sure he was glad to see you."

"He was. We talked a lot, and I tried to get him to tell me what's been going on. I let him know I wasn't pleased with his shoplifting, and I hope my talking to him will influence him not to do it again."

"Did his father show up for his birthday?"

Frank frowned, tossing dirty socks into his room. "No, he didn't show up. He didn't even call." He shook his head. "He's such a lousy dad. I don't know what Trish was thinking when she married that loser."

She fingered the empty scotch bottle sitting on the coffee table. "Did you go to the liquor store to buy scotch?" Her voice wavered, and she continued to look around the room. Empty beer bottles and a half-empty bottle of wine sat on the end table.

He took the bottle away from her and dropped it into the trash. "I told you things have been hectic in my life lately." A hard edge crept into his voice, and he continued to gather items and place them in the garbage can.

Clothes were strewn all over the place, and the hamper overflowed with garments. She wondered when he had last done his laundry. After he placed the paper bag in a kitchen cupboard, he pulled two cups from the cabinet and put several cubes of ice into each. The ice popped when he poured the lemonade. Emily sat on the couch, and he handed her the cup. She took a drink, closing her eyes, relishing the sweet, tangy taste of the lemonade and the clean citrus scent of Frank's cologne. "You made this?"

He chuckled. "Yes, I made it."

She raised her eyebrows, enjoying another sip. "It's good."

"Thanks. All it is, is fresh lemons, sugar, and water." He shrugged. "It's no big deal." Silence filled the room, and Emily drained her glass. "Would you like more lemonade?"

"Please."

He returned to the kitchen with her empty glass so he could refill it. As he performed the chore, she was about to ask him about the audit when she noticed the wedding picture sitting on the coffee table.

She lifted the photo and saw Frank wearing a gray tuxedo, and his arm was around a bride. The woman's skin was the color of ripe blackberries, and her dark hair shimmered over her shoulders. Her arm was casually draped around Frank's waist, and her laughter seemed to jump right out of the picture.

She clutched the picture as he returned with the lemonade.

"You're married?" Her voice wavered.

He shook his head. "I guess I should have mentioned it sooner. She's dead." He placed the picture on the coffee table face down.

She stared at the down-turned picture frame. "Dead?"

"My wife is dead. She was killed about a year ago."

"Killed, a year ago? That's so recent."

"I know. I still think about her a lot."

So many questions filled her mind that she didn't know which to ask first. "She's very pretty."

"Yes, Julie was very beautiful."

Silence, thick and heavy, filled the room. She wondered what had happened to Frank's wife. "How long were you two married?"

"Two years."

"I'm sorry."

He stood and walked to the window, parting the curtains. Light streamed into the room from the streetlamps. "You know, I'm so sick of hearing that."

She stood beside him. "Hearing what?" Tears glistened in his eyes, and he quickly turned away. "What's wrong?"

When he didn't initially respond, Emily was tempted to let the subject drop.

He wiped his eyes and dropped the curtain, returning to the couch. Emily joined him, still wondering about the death of his wife. "I miss my wife so much. It's one of the reasons I've started drinking again."

"I think your pain will lessen with time."

"I killed her, Emily. I killed my wife."

"I know you couldn't have killed her."

"It's my fault she's dead."

She touched his shoulder. "What happened?"

"Julie was raised in foster care."

She recalled the sad stories she'd heard about children in foster care. "That sounds rough."

"Yeah, but since she had been through so much with her brother during the time they were in foster care, they were closer than they should have been."

"What do you mean?"

"Her brother was into drugs. At one point, he owed somebody over a thousand dollars."

"Did she loan him the money?"

Frank chuckled, the sarcastic sound echoing in the room. "It could hardly be called a loan, because I knew he would never pay us back. I didn't understand why she kept bailing him out."

"So did she give him the money?"

"I told her not to. She promised me she wouldn't meet him in that dangerous neighborhood where he lived to give him the money."

"But she went to meet with her brother anyway."

He nodded, tears falling down his cheeks. "Yeah, she went. Some stuff went down, and there was a bust when she was there. She was accidentally shot and died a few days later."

She hugged him, silently praying she could say the right words. "Did they catch the person who shot her?" she asked, ending their embrace.

"Yeah, they caught him, and he's in prison. But I tell you what, if they hadn't caught him, I'd be going after him myself. I would have searched until I found her killer if the police hadn't gotten to him first."

"Why do you think this is your fault?"

"I should have realized what she was going to do. I should have gone with her. I knew how stubborn she was about helping her brother. Maybe I could have talked her out of it. If I'd reasoned with her, she may not have gone to meet with him and she'd still be alive."

"Or she could have thought about this with a level head."

He gave her a strange look. "What do you mean?"

"I know you miss your wife, and I can see how much you loved her, but it wasn't your job to ensure she always thought rationally. You're beating yourself up over something you had no control over. Julie knew what kind of crowd her brother hung out with, and I'm sure she knew about the danger of meeting him in that seedy area. Why couldn't she have figured out another way to get him the money? Could she have mailed him a check—"

"The type of people he dealt with wouldn't be waiting on a check."

Emily shrugged, still not deterred from making Frank see reason. "You mentioned to me that you were mad at your parents."

He nodded. "My anger at my parents started years ago when I'd started dating Julie. They didn't like the fact that she wasn't from a good family, and they didn't support my marriage."

"Is that the only reason you're angry with them?"

"Emily, when my parents rejected my wife, it was like they were rejecting me, too. I'll be honest with you and let you know that my parents did do something else besides reject Julie."

"What did they do?"

"When I got engaged to Julie, they did a background check on her and her brother. They didn't think she'd be a suitable addition to the family, so they told me the only way they would support my marriage would be if I made her sign a prenup."

Emily gasped. "A prenup? Do you mean a prenuptial agreement?"

He nodded. "Yes. They felt like she was just a gold digger, wanting to get into the family to get some of their fortune."

"You didn't ask her to sign it, did you?"

He shook his head. "No, I loved her, and I couldn't hurt her like that. When we got married, she wondered about the distant relationship we had with my parents. She was smart enough to know that my parents' cold reception of her was tied to her background, but she never knew about the prenup."

"So they didn't talk to Julie much at all?"

He shook his head. "Not really. It was awful. When they distanced themselves from my wife, my relationship with them changed. When Julie died, they offered no sympathy. I feel like they thought she deserved what happened to her."

"Frank! Are you sure about this?"

He shook his head. "They never said it, but they just acted like they didn't care when she died. They didn't call or anything."

"Maybe they thought you didn't want them to call. Maybe they didn't want to make you angrier."

"You sound like you're defending them."

She touched his arm. "I'm just trying to make you see this rationally. What does Trish say about all this?"

"She says my parents want to start speaking to me again."

She said the first thing that came to her mind. "You'll need to forgive your parents for the way they mistreated your wife. I've told you this before, but the only One who can help you is God."

He gave her an icy stare. "What?"

"What about your faith in God? Haven't you prayed about your pain, asked God to help you forgive Julie's killer and to forgive your parents?" She gestured around the cluttered room. "You can't drown your sorrows with booze."

"I don't care about God, and God doesn't care about me."

"How can you say that when you're not giving Him a chance?"

He huffed, running his fingers over his head. "Julie was saved not long after we were married. She tried to get me to accept Christ."

"What happened?"

His voice thickened. "Julie got killed." His dark eyes stared into hers. "I can't forget about that and accept God."

She prayed that God would lead her to say the right words. "Julie was saved? She's with Jesus now. Remember that."

He clasped his hands together. "Don't be preaching to me." He gave her a scathing look. "Besides, you have no idea what I've been through this past year."

She stood and stepped back, startled by his sudden outburst. She swallowed, her anger brewing like a slow stew simmering to boil. "I just lost my father, and I lost my mother years ago!" She clenched her hands together. "I know what it's like to lose someone you love." She calmed down before she squeezed his hand. "Give God a chance. I still have the church program from last week's service in my purse," she said, opening her purse and pulling out the program and a pen. She circled one of the contact numbers on the back. "The information about the alcoholic support group at my church is on the back." She pressed the paper into his palm. "The worship services are also listed. Devon Crandall is the leader for the alcoholic support group. They have weekly meetings, and I've heard good things about his work with the ministry."

He placed the program on the coffee table. "I'll think about it."

"I'll be praying for you, Frank." Emily embraced him before she left.

&

The following Sunday, Frank awakened and sat up in bed, cradling his aching head. "Oh, man." The empty liquor bottle stared back at him, mocking his mistake. His sour stomach churned, and before long he ran to the bathroom and threw up. He relaxed against the cool, white-tiled wall, willing his rapidly beating heart to slow down. "God, I can't go on like this. I just can't." The nightmare about Julie haunted him again the previous night, and he squeezed his eyes shut, willing the unpleasant dream to vanish from his mind.

His cell phone chirped, and he stood on wobbly legs and plodded into the bedroom. He pulled the black instrument from the shelf. Not bothering to check the caller ID, he flipped the phone open. "Hello."

"Hi, little brother."

"Trish." The last thing he needed was a lecture from his sister.

"My goodness, don't sound so happy to hear from me." Sarcasm dripped from her voice, and Frank plopped back onto the bed.

"I'm not feeling great right now."

"You're probably hungover."

He winced, ashamed of his nightly routine. "Are Mark and Regina okay?"

"The kids are fine. I didn't call to talk about them or about your drinking problem. I wanted to talk about Dad."

"What about him?" He cradled the phone between his ear and shoulder, grabbing the large bottle of acetaminophen on his bedside table. Popping the jar open, he shook four tablets into his palm and dropped them into his mouth. He drank from a bottle of water, swallowing the pills.

"He's still sick."

"Has he been to the doctor yet?"

She scoffed. "You know he hasn't. But he was telling me the other day that he wished you would talk to them again."

He shook his head, but the movement caused bullets of pain to shoot behind his eyes. Taking a deep breath, he laid back on the pillows. "I don't have time to listen to this."

"Well, you better make time. I think if you'd talk to Dad again, he might feel better. Maybe he'll be so glad to hear from you that he'll do whatever you ask him to, even if that's going to the doctor."

Still holding the phone, he entered the kitchen, willing his aching head to stop pounding. He opened the cupboard. The canister of coffee beckoned him. He removed the can and opened it, spilling coffee grounds into the white filter. "Trish, I have to go now."

"But Frank—"

"I'll talk to you later." He snapped his phone shut, throwing it on the kitchen table. Soon drops of coffee splattered into the coffeemaker, filling the kitchen with an aromatic scent. He pulled a mug from the cupboard and filled it with the steaming brew, along with a generous portion of cream and sugar.

He entered his living room and sat on the couch. Waves of guilt washed over him, and he blinked away unshed tears. He turned away from the wedding photo, continuing to sip his coffee. As the caffeine soothed his nerves, he set his mug down and returned to his bedroom. He found a box of his belongings, which he had never unpacked, sitting on the bottom of the closet. He dumped the contents, riffling through trinkets, old magazines, and books. Finally, he spotted his large black Bible, a gift from his deceased wife, among the clutter. Once he'd returned to the living room, he retrieved his mug, still holding his Bible. The old church program Emily had given him that week still sat on the coffee table.

He gazed at the paper, making his decision.

❧

An hour later, Frank sat in a pew at Monkton Christian Church. Once the sermon finished, Frank mulled over the pastor's words about forgiveness. Waves of heat washed over him when he stepped outside. People scurried to their cars, anxious to avoid the dreaded high temperatures.

He glanced around the sea of brown faces and stopped when he spotted Emily. Her white dress cascaded over her slim brown body, and her dark tresses were pulled into a severe ponytail, accenting her high cheekbones and full lips.

Kelly and Christine stood beside Emily. Laughter floated

from the three women, and he wondered what they were talking about. Emily lifted her head, looking directly at him. Her smile faltered.

"Hi, Emily." He then gazed at Kelly and Christine. "Nice seeing you again, Kelly, Christine."

Kelly and Christine said hello. A mischievous smile played on Kelly's full lips, and after a few more words to Emily, Kelly took her exit. "I hope she didn't leave because of me," Frank commented.

"No, she's meeting somebody."

Christine spoke up. "I need to go, too. There's a sale going on at some of the stores at the Inner Harbor, and I was going to go and look around."

Emily touched Christine's shoulder. "Is everything okay? I don't want you going shopping, buying things you can't afford just to make yourself feel better."

Christine shook her head. "I didn't lose my job, but I just discovered they only went through the first round of layoffs. They're going to do more within the next couple of weeks." She shrugged. "Maybe I'll just look around the stores and not buy anything."

"Did you want to share lunch with me instead?"

Christine declined and bid them farewell.

They stood awkwardly on the hot sidewalk, and Emily spoke. "I was shocked to see you here today."

Frank didn't comment on her observation. People walked around them, and she touched his arm, leaning in a bit closer. "You don't look like you feel very well, and your eyes are red. Are you sick?" Frank sighed, unsure of how to respond "Did you have too much to drink last night?"

He pulled his arm away. "I don't want to talk about that right now."

"Is there something else you wanted to talk to me about?"

He touched her arm. "I never got a chance to talk to you about the audit the other day when you came to my apartment."

"Oh, I'd forgotten all about that with everything you told me." She clutched the strap of her purse. "I'm getting ready to eat lunch. I could call you this afternoon if you want."

"Were you going out to eat?"

"Kelly, Christine, and I were planning to go to the Monkton Village Market for lunch, but they bailed on me. Christine is pressed to go to this sale, and I don't have the energy to go shopping with her. She shops for hours! So we could go and get something to eat if you wanted."

They drove to the vegetarian restaurant and entered. Emily ordered pancakes with fruit, a blueberry muffin, and a cup of tea. Frank's stomach was still sour, so he purchased a bottle of water. He took out his wallet to pay for their food, telling the cashier their order was together. Once they'd sat at their table, Emily said, "You didn't have to pay for my meal."

He waved her comment away. "This is a business meal anyway."

Emily bowed her head and blessed her food. Her long lashes fluttered when she opened her eyes.

"I'm surprised you're eating at a vegetarian place," Frank said.

"It's just a change of pace. I've eaten at just about every place in Monkton since Laura's been gone. They don't have many places to eat here, and you know that I'm tired of making sandwiches every day."

"Speaking of your stepmother, do you know when she's getting back?" He couldn't keep the anxiety out of his voice.

Emily raised her eyebrows, her dark eyes full of suspicion. "Why do you ask?"

"I needed to talk to her about something important. I can call her, but I'd rather talk to her in person."

"What's wrong? Is the audit not going well?"

"It's not going well at all."

"What's happened?"

He thought about the latest development. "The numbers don't add up."

She frowned, staring into his eyes. "What do you mean?"

"There's something wrong. There are large amounts of cash that are unaccounted for."

She put her fork aside. "So there's money missing?"

He ran his fingers over his head, frustrated. "Yes. When you e-mailed me those missing documents, I was able to piece this information together. I'm still trying to figure out what your father's done. I was wondering if your stepmother might know something."

Emily pushed her plate away. "I doubt it. I already told you we didn't know much about the finances of our farm." She appeared pensive as she continued to speak. "Laura and I are lousy with numbers."

He frowned. "Really?"

"Yes. Back in grade school and even in college I struggled with math courses. The only reason I was able to graduate with my bachelor's and master's was because I hired a private tutor to help me with all my math classes. I can barely balance a checkbook."

"You're kidding."

She shook her head. "No, I'm not kidding. I've struggled with math my entire life, and Laura told me she's never been good with math, either. My dad had this natural mathematical ability, so we just let him handle all the money. You probably wouldn't understand since you crunch numbers all day."

His mathematical abilities had always come naturally, so it was hard to understand how someone couldn't balance a checkbook. He touched her hand. "Don't worry about it. I'm sure there's some explanation. Did you find your father's missing tax returns?"

"No, not yet. I've been looking during my spare time." She

told him they'd been baling hay recently and the intense heat had been affecting the corn crop. "I've been busy on the farm a lot, and I've also been thankful that one or both of the brothers have been showing up for both the evening and morning milkings."

They sat in silence for a few minutes before Emily began eating her pancakes again and Frank drank his water. Her lovely voice broke the silence. "Have you been okay? You have circles under your eyes."

He set his water bottle back on the table. "Remember you told me about Devon Crandall?"

"Yes, I remember."

"I showed up to a meeting." Her startled eyes met his. "But I couldn't go in."

"Why not?"

"I just couldn't. I stood outside the door for a minute, and I don't think anybody saw me." He gazed out the window at a couple who walked by holding hands. "Maybe I can give up the alcohol on my own."

"You told me that you'd had alcohol problems before when you were in college. How were you able to quit back then?"

He recalled that time in his life. "They had AA meetings near campus. But. . ."

She grabbed his hand. "But what?"

"To tell you the truth, I've been doing some heavy drinking for over a year now. Back when I was in college, I'd only been drinking for a few months before it started becoming a problem. I think it might be harder for me to quit this time."

"Maybe you should give it another try. Maybe you could have somebody go to the meeting with you."

"Going to that group of people makes me nervous."

"Why?"

"I don't know."

"Devon is an understanding man. Maybe you can just meet with him to talk about what you've been going through."

As she ate her lunch, Frank gave Emily's advice serious thought.

eight

During the next month, Emily's days continued to be filled with farm chores. She was glad when they had almost two straight days of rain. The claps of thunder and bursts of lightning thrilled her, making her giddy. The heat and dry weather had worried her, and the moisture was just what her crops needed to thrive.

She'd called Laura about Frank's questions, but her step-mother was shocked to hear about the missing money. As far as Laura knew, all of her father's financial information was in his office. Laura had mentioned it was certainly possible that there were files elsewhere in the house, so Emily said she'd keep looking around to see if she could find any missing documents that would help account for the missing funds.

One morning when the milking was done, Emily and Jeremy stood at the sink, rinsing the equipment and cleaning the barn. The slender teen turned toward Emily. "My mom told me to ask if your mother was coming home soon."

"She said she was coming home shortly. I've been talking to her every day." She glanced at him, wondering if he understood the pain of losing somebody so close. "I don't want to keep bothering her about when she's coming home. But I do miss her a lot." She gave the teen a smile and continued rinsing her equipment. She was a little hurt that Laura had not called to wish her a happy birthday. "Make sure either you or your brother or both of you are here tonight to milk the cows."

"Oh, we'll both be here." He held up a cell phone. "You can even call us to make sure we're here if you want to."

A few hours later, Kelly and Christine arrived at Emily's farm, and the three women rode to the state fair together. When they arrived on the fairgrounds, they assisted the rest of Monkton Christian Church's hospitality committee. In addition to serving pound cake and bottled water, they'd planned on doing face painting to entice the children to their booth. After working all morning, Emily was ready for a break.

"Hi, Emily." Frank's voice greeted her ears like a soothing lullaby. Turning toward him, she enjoyed the sensations that skittered across her skin when he touched her arm. "Frank. I didn't know you'd be here."

"The fair was advertised in the church bulletin, and you told me you were on the committee." His dark eyes sparkled. "Can you take a break?"

She checked her watch. "Is it okay if I take my lunch break now?"

Kelly completed a child's face painting. "Why don't you go ahead with Frank and have a good time." She reached for her purse beneath the booth. "If you don't mind, you can bring me back something to eat." She told her what she wanted for lunch. The rest of the committee members also produced money for lunches since they weren't interested in walking around the fair.

Frank and Emily strolled away from the booth. "Why did you come to the fair?"

"I came to see you. Since I haven't been coming out to your farm lately, I've missed you."

His words warmed her heart, and she decided to be truthful with him. "I've missed you, too."

They strolled around the grounds then bought hot dogs from a vendor and sat at one of the picnic tables. She bit into her hot dog and drank some soda. "How have you been?" she asked.

"I've been okay." He stared at the crowd populating the fairgrounds. "Well, I wish I could be better."

She took a deep breath before asking her next question. "Have you been drinking?"

"I've been working late, and that helps a little bit, but it doesn't keep me away from the alcohol."

"Did you call Devon Crandall?"

"No."

"Why not? He's very easygoing, and I'm sure he wouldn't mind if you called him." He failed to respond. "Are you coming to church again tomorrow?"

He smiled before sipping his soda. "Yes, I plan on going."

"You should try and talk to Devon after church tomorrow. He's one of the ushers. He's well over six feet tall with gray hair. His wife is so short that they look funny together because of his height."

"Okay, I'll keep that in mind."

She bit into her hot dog. "How are Mark and Regina doing? Does Mark still call you a lot?"

He grinned. "Thanks for asking. Both of them are doing fine. Mark has been calling me just about every day. If I don't hear from him, I'll usually call. I'm glad he hasn't gotten into any more trouble, and he seems excited to be back in school."

"I'm glad to hear they're doing well." She observed the colorful tents on the grounds for a few seconds. "Oh, Frank, I almost forgot to tell you." She abandoned her hot dog and clenched her hands together.

"What's wrong?"

"Nothing's wrong. This morning I found the tax returns you were looking for. There were also some other bank statements, too."

He frowned, finishing his food. "Other bank statements? What kind of account is it? Is it checking, savings, money market?"

She shrugged. "I'm not sure."

"Were they to another account, a different one than the one I was looking at?"

"I think so. I didn't realize he had an account there. This bank is all the way on the other side of Baltimore County."

"Did you check the balance? Maybe that's where the missing funds are."

She told him the sum that was in the account.

His eyes widened. "Whoa. Why would he separate that much money into another account? It must be either a money market, savings, or retirement account."

"You know, it's the strangest thing. . ."

He sipped his soda. "What?"

"I didn't find them in his office."

Frank frowned again. "Where did you find them?"

"They were stuck in a manila folder in the hall closet." She shook her head. "I don't understand why he had all his other tax returns on his computer with the exception of those two. Why would he separate them like that?"

He wiped his mouth with a napkin. "I'm not sure. If you don't mind, I'd like for you to scan them and e-mail them to me as soon as possible. That way I can complete the work for your farm."

Questions popped through her brain. If Frank finished his audit for their farm, did that mean she would have no contact with him anymore? He touched her hand. "What's the matter?"

She shook her head, not wanting to voice her concerns. "Nothing. I'm okay."

When they were finished with their lunch, they strolled the fairgrounds again. Frank walked back with her to the booth before he left the event. Christine and Kelly immediately surrounded her, wanting to know what was going on between her and Frank.

❧

"What's wrong, Emily?" asked Christine as they pulled into her driveway.

Emily shook her head. "Nothing's wrong. I'm just tired."

Gravel crunched beneath their feet as they walked to the front door. Emily yawned, looking forward to getting into her soft bed and going to sleep. She stopped walking, looking at her friends. "Do you guys really feel like visiting right now? I was going to go to bed."

Christine patted her shoulder. "We'll try not to wear you out too much. Let's make some coffee and talk for a bit."

Kelly agreed. "Yes, a cup of coffee sounds like a good idea."

Emily walked up the steps, concerned about the full darkness cloaking her house since she usually left the porch light on. She made a mental note to change the lightbulb. The hinges on the screen door creaked as she entered.

"Happy birthday!" The dark kitchen flooded with light, and a sea of familiar faces filled the room.

Emily placed her hand against her mouth. "Oh my goodness."

"Hey, Emily!" Laura Cooper strolled into the kitchen.

"Mom!" Emily shrieked, pulling the older woman into an embrace. The familiar scent of Laura's jasmine perfume filled Emily with euphoria, and tears gathered in her eyes.

Kelly pressed a tissue into Emily's hand. "Happy birthday, Emily!"

She glanced at Kelly and Christine. "You two kept this from me all day!"

Emily released her mother, wiping her eyes. "Mom, you look thinner since you left."

Laura swatted Emily's arm. "I've been fine."

Emily shook her head, still trying to take in the whole atmosphere. "I was wondering why you didn't call me today!" She ignored the numerous guests, eager to speak with Laura.

"Honey, you know I wanted to call you today, but I can't keep secrets. I know I would've accidentally said something to spoil Kelly and Christine's surprise!"

Emily's joy bubbled to the surface, almost gushing forward. Crepe paper streamers fluttered when the wind blew in from the open screen door.

Emily stared at the crowd, touched. "This is one of the biggest surprises I've received in my entire life."

A strong, unique scent filled the air, and Emily rushed over to the stove, opening the lid on one of the pots. "You made me chitterlings!" The pig intestines, cooked to perfection, were one of her favorite foods. Serving herself, she piled some on a plate and placed a generous amount of mustard on the side. She took a bite, savoring the flavor.

Her friends from church were present as well as Cameron. As she continued to eat her food, Christine took her aside. "I'm sorry about Cameron coming."

"Why is he here?" asked Emily.

Christine rolled her eyes. "When we were at the grocery store getting the stuff for the party, Cameron was nearby and we didn't realize it. He overheard us talking about your party, and he asked if he could come. I couldn't tell him no."

Later, when she opened the gifts, she was pleased to see the assortment of perfumes and lotions people gave her. She also received some gift cards to her favorite clothing store. However, she was shocked Cameron gave her pearl earrings. "Thanks, Cameron," she said, giving him a small smile.

The party lasted until well into the night. Once the guests were gone and Christine and Kelly had put away the leftovers, it was close to midnight, but Emily was still high on energy. She sat on the porch with her stepmother on the large swing. They swayed in the gentle summer breeze, and Emily was happy to have Laura home again. "How's Lisa doing?"

"She's fine. We had a nice visit."

"Has Becky been calling you much?"

Laura looked away for a few seconds. "You know how strained things are between Becky and me. She calls every few weeks. I just wish we could settle our differences and have a better relationship. I've been praying for a better relationship with both daughters for a long time, so I'm hoping things can change between us."

Emily patted Laura's shoulder, praying things worked out with her girls. She knew Laura had divorced at a young age and her ex-husband had been granted custody of their two small children. Her husband had hired a good lawyer, and he'd used Laura's past convictions with drugs against her. She'd cleaned her life up by the time she was married and had children, but her husband's lawyer was able to convince the judge that the father would be a better parent because he'd never had the substance abuse problems Laura had had in the past. Laura had told her that she always regretted losing custody of her children, even though she had generous visitation rights. Her daughters were now in their early thirties, and she wondered if the strained relationship they had was due to the fact that Laura did not raise them herself.

Even though they'd talked about it on the phone, she told Laura about the audit and about finding her father's tax returns. "Mom, we really should have been more involved in the financial side of things," Emily commented as the swing continued to sway.

Laura touched Emily's hand. "Honey, I know we should have. But there's nothing we can do but move forward."

Emily again mentioned the correspondence Frank had found with a Realtor in her father's files. "He said it appeared as if he was planning to sell the farm. I told him he must be mistaken. Are you sure Dad never mentioned this to you?"

Her stepmother remained silent as the swing continued to rock.

"Mom, what are you hiding?"

"Honey, I wasn't completely honest with you when you mentioned this to me before. I didn't want to tell you this, but Frank is right. Shortly before your father died, he was contemplating selling this farm."

Emily's mouth dropped open. "But. . .why? Daddy always loved farming!"

"I know, but he confided to me that for the last two years profits had been bad for the farm."

Emily shook her head. "I don't believe it. Why didn't he ever say anything to me about this?"

She touched Emily's arm. "He didn't want you to worry about it, that's why."

"But, I still don't understand. Frank would have said something about our farm not being profitable, wouldn't he?"

"Emily, remember he's not finished auditing the books." She frowned.

"What's wrong, Mom?"

"I didn't want to tell you this, but. . .before your father passed, I could see how much the financial strain of the farm was bothering him. I tried to get him to hire an accountant to go through his tax returns and stuff to see if he may have been missing some important write-offs."

"And he didn't agree to do it, right?"

"He reacted worse than you did when I made my suggestion. He got angry with me. You were at a church function that night, and we argued about it for hours. Honey, your father was good with numbers, but he was not an accountant and he was no CPA. I know we hear about farms selling out sometimes, but I knew there were farms that did pretty well. I figured if he got advice from an accountant, he may have gotten an even better return when he filed his taxes and when he invested his money. You always hear about tax laws changing and such, and I wanted him to see a professional about his farm."

Emily rubbed her head. "Is this why you wanted Frank to audit our books?"

Laura nodded. "Yes. I've been worried about this for a long time, and since Paul is gone, I'm even more worried about it. We seem to be making it financially day by day, but I just want to make sure your father knew what he was doing when he accounted for this farm and when he filed his taxes in the past."

This newfound information made Emily's head ache. She silently prayed for strength before deciding to tell her mother something else that was on her mind. "Mom, I think I have a big problem."

"What is it? Has something else happened since I've been gone?"

"Well, you know I've been spending some time with Frank."

"You like him, don't you?"

"Yes, how did you know?"

"You say his name like you're familiar with him. I know he has feelings for you, too."

"How do you know that?"

"Just from talking to him on the phone. He seems concerned about the farm, more concerned than a stranger should be. When I speak to him, I feel like I'm talking to a friend." They were silent for a few minutes as they continued to rock on the swing. "Maybe the Lord is trying to tell you it's time to move on since your engagement to Jamal ended."

"I don't think so." They rocked well into the night, and she told her mother all about why Frank was the wrong man for her.

❧

"God will never leave you nor forsake you. I want all of you to remember that when you leave church today," said Pastor Brown to the congregation. Frank closed his Bible, still thinking about the words. He sat in the pew beside Emily and her mother. After all these weeks, he'd finally gotten to meet Laura.

When the service ended, Emily took Frank's hand, causing sparks of delight to dance through his fingers. She gestured toward Laura. "We're going out to lunch at the Wagon Wheel. Did you want to come with us?"

Frank shook his head. He glanced at the ushers still in the back of the church.

"In case you're interested, Devon Crandall is the one on the left," she told him.

He squeezed her hand. "Thanks," he mumbled. Emily and Laura exited the church, and Frank swallowed, still working up the courage to approach the older man. He breathed deeply as he walked up to the usher. "Devon Crandall?" The man gazed at Frank, his dark eyes warm and friendly.

"Yes?"

"My name is Franklin Reese."

The usher smiled, shaking Frank's hand. "I've noticed you coming to our church recently. It's hard not to notice a new member in a church this small."

Frank sighed, not wanting Devon to get the wrong idea. "Well, I'm not a member of this church."

"If you're a member of God's family, then that makes you a member of this church."

"No, I don't think I'm a member of God's family, either."

The man's smile faded, and he squeezed Frank's hand. "You look like you need somebody to talk to, son."

"I don't want to hold you up."

"There's no hold up." He placed his hands on his hips, continuing to assess Frank. "People are always telling me how perceptive I am, and right about now I think you need a friend. Would you like to come to my house for lunch?"

"I don't want to bother you."

"Oh, it's no bother. My wife usually cooks too much food anyway." He patted his gut. "I certainly don't need those extra calories."

"Okay."

Devon beamed. "Good. I'll just let my wife know you're coming. You can follow us to our house."

A half hour later, Frank shared lunch with Devon and his wife. The tiny salt-and-pepper-haired woman welcomed Frank into her home, embracing him warmly. When he'd commuted to the Crandalls' house, his queasy stomach had settled from his drinking binge the night before, and he was able to enjoy the tasty pot roast, mashed potatoes, and green salad. "You and Devon can have your dessert in the library," suggested Devon's wife. After placing coffee and cake on a silver tray and carrying it into the library, she left, saying she had some things to do around the house.

The blinds were open, and bright sunlight spilled into the room.

"So, tell me, Franklin—"

"You can call me Frank."

"Okay, Frank. Tell me why you approached me in church."

Frank stirred his coffee, wondering where to start. Did he explain the anger he had for his parents and the death of his wife, which drove him to drink? Did he tell of his budding feelings for Emily? "Since Paul Cooper died, Laura and Emily needed help with their bookkeeping. They contacted my employer, and I was sent to do the job. Emily mentioned you ran an alcoholic support group."

Devon nodded, serving the cake. "Yes, I do. I've been running it for over ten years. The group is not just for members of our church; it's also there for people in surrounding churches. We meet every week in the basement of the church."

"I know." He mentioned showing up at the meeting the previous week but refusing to enter the room.

Devon didn't seem surprised about Frank's actions. "You made it to the meeting, so that's a big step. You should come in next time. We'd be glad to have you. So, tell me what's been making you drink."

"My parents never accepted my wife because of her background. My family's pretty wealthy, and my parents thought they knew who would be the best wife for me. They didn't support my marriage, and when my wife died, they never apologized for not accepting Julie into the family." He briefly told of how Julie was killed, and then he added, "I felt so bad, Devon. Not only did I lose my wife, but. . ." He looked away and didn't realize tears streamed from his eyes until Devon gave him a tissue. "I lost a child." He shook his head. "A few days before Julie died, she told me she was pregnant." He wiped his wet eyes and blew his nose. "I just wish there was some way I could've stopped her from going to meet her brother that day." He balled his hands into fists. "I feel so bad. The alcohol is the only thing that makes me feel better anymore." Devon squeezed Frank's shoulder.

Once Frank was calmer, Devon asked him a question. "When does the urge to drink happen?"

Frank was truthful, telling Devon the urge usually hit in the evening, after working a full day.

"Frank, I'll be praying for you every day, but you really need to meet with the alcoholic support group weekly." He gave Frank a business card. "You can call me anytime you want to, but I'm warning you, I'll be calling you every day, too." He stroked his chin. "By coming to me, I think you've admitted to yourself that you have a problem. Also, I want to point out that you can't handle this sort of problem alone. Not only do you need help from the support group, but you need to find help in Jesus. If you'll just accept Him as your Savior, then the load you carry on your shoulders will become lighter. Remember what the pastor said this morning: Jesus will never leave you nor forsake you."

Frank certainly felt left and forsaken, but he didn't know if he'd find the courage to surrender his life to Jesus.

nine

A few days later Frank met with his boss and informed him of his final discovery for the Coopers' farm. "You'll need to meet with the wife since she's the one who initiated the audit," his boss had advised.

Now Frank sat in his car in front of the Coopers' farm. It was midafternoon, and he was scheduled to meet with Laura Cooper alone. When he'd called that morning to make the appointment, she'd said to come that afternoon since Emily would be at the grocery store. His thoughts wandered to the previous night. The urge to drink had slammed into him after Trish called, again saying that their father was not doing so well. He'd picked up the phone to call his dad but found the old anger festering in his heart like a canker sore. Instead of turning to drink, he'd called Devon Crandall, who'd again stressed that Frank needed to find relief in Jesus. Devon had encouraged him to come to the next support group meeting, and he'd also told him to discover more about God. "Read the New Testament, Frank. It'll tell you about Jesus' nature." He'd spoken to the man for more than an hour. After tossing and turning in bed for a long time, he'd finally gone to sleep—without taking a drink of alcohol.

He got out of the car and walked to the screen door. The urge to drink almost consumed him, but he forced himself to think of Emily, the Cooper farm, and the news he had to deliver. Taking a deep breath, he rapped on the door. Laura sat at the table, reading her Bible and drinking a cup of coffee. The woman looked up, smiling. "Frank." She placed a marker in her Bible and closed it. "Frank, come on in." When he sat at the table, she touched his hand. "You seem a bit agitated. Are you okay?"

"Not really."

"Is something wrong?"

"I'm fine. I wanted to talk to you about the audit. I don't think Emily looked through all the financial papers in that file she found."

"What are you talking about?"

"Your husband had Excel spreadsheets keeping track of winnings and losses at a gambling casino over in Delaware. I've found evidence that he was spending large sums of the farm's profits at a casino. He kept records of what he had spent and how much he owed the farm from his gambling debts."

Laura cried softly. "I thought he had stopped gambling. He was going to a support group."

Her reaction caught him off guard. "You knew about this?"

"Yes, he did this a long time ago, but he promised me he'd stopped. I can now see it was all a lie." Frank found a box of tissues on the counter, and he gave them to her.

"Emily doesn't know?"

"No, neither of his daughters knew about their father's bad habit. I didn't think it was necessary to tell them since he'd told me he'd stopped."

If Emily and Laura wanted to start keeping track of the accounting records and tracking the profitability of the farm, then he didn't see how he could hide this information from Emily. He relayed his concerns to Laura.

"I understand. I just don't know how to break it to her. She thought her father was perfect." She blew her nose and looked at him as if to seek comfort. "I don't know how I'm going to tell Emily. But I don't have a choice." She sniffed. "Oh, Lord, please help me."

"Mrs. Cooper, that's not all I needed to tell you. I believe your husband falsified his tax returns."

With shaky hands, she covered her mouth, continuing to cry. "Do you mean he owes money to the government?"

"Yes. He grossly understated his revenue, and I know he owes the IRS some money. . .a lot of money. He's falsified his tax returns for the last two years." He told her how he couldn't find the tax returns for the last two years and that Emily found them hidden in the closet. "Did you look at the tax returns before you signed them?"

"Paul took care of all the finances. When he told me to sign the tax returns, I just trusted the numbers were accurate." She wiped her tears away. "Will we have to lose the farm to pay the back taxes? This farm means so much to Emily. She would die if she lost this home."

"You could lose your farm. But you'll have to let her know what happened. Usually in situations like this, the IRS will want their money back. They might work with you and Emily to set up a payment plan or something." When she had pulled herself together, he finally spoke again. "When are you going to tell Emily?"

She wiped her nose. "I'll tell her before the end of the day. She deserves to know."

He tried to make her feel better. "Mrs. Cooper, I think your husband may have been keeping track of all this because he was planning on replacing the money he lost back into the farm."

She nodded. "He's done this before, a long time ago. He thought if he kept at it long enough, he would win the money back. But sometimes, when he did win back the money he'd lost, the temptation to gamble it away again was just too great." She shook her head. "I'll never understand why this happened, but I promise I'll talk to Emily about it today."

❧

Later that day Emily returned from the barn, and fatigue washed through her. She told Laura she was going to take a short nap before doing the evening milking. Sleep consumed her until the phone rang. Emily turned her head on the soft pillow, snuggling deeper into her blankets, hoping to get a few more minutes of sleep before milking time.

Laura's footsteps pounded on the floor, and Emily's door flew open when she entered. "Emily, you've got to wake up." She opened the blinds, and sunlight spilled into the room. Emily regretfully broke her midday nap. "Mom, what's wrong?"

Laura paced the room, her mouth set in a grim line. "Becky's had her baby! They just gave her a C-section at the hospital."

Emily's world tilted, and she sent up a silent plea to God for her stepsister's health and for the baby. "But she's only seven months pregnant. What happened?"

"They think the size of her fibroids caused her to go into early labor." Her stepmother shook her head. She sat on the bed and grabbed Emily's hand, closing her eyes. "Lord, please be with us during this trying time." Her voice filled the room as they lifted up the plight of Becky's baby. When their prayer was finished, she squeezed Emily's hand.

"They say the baby's chances of survival are good." Her mother shook her head. "I've got to get out there."

Emily's heart filled with dread at the thought of Laura leaving again, but she knew it was for the best. "I know you do, Mom."

"I hate leaving you so soon."

Emily shook her head, patting Laura's frail shoulder. "Don't feel bad about it. Becky's got two other children, and since it's the busy season at Keith's job, you know he's going to be working some serious overtime now." Both of Becky's children were under five, so her stepmother would have her hands full. "Don't overdo it, Mom. I don't want your back to go out on you again." The last time that had happened, she'd been in bed for a week, barely able to move without being in pain.

"Honey, I won't." She glanced at the clock. "Since Becky's

had a C-section, I know it's going to be hard for her to get around for about a week or so. I want to try and get a flight out of here today."

One of Laura's friends from church soon arrived to take her to the airport. Emily was sorry to see her stepmother go so soon after returning from her trip to Florida, but she knew it was necessary for her to be there to assist her daughter with her children.

That evening Emily was out in the barn with Darren milking the cows when her cell phone chirped. She told Darren to continue milking alone for a few minutes and flipped the phone open. "Hi, Laura."

"Emily, with all the excitement about Becky's baby, I forgot to tell you about Frank's audit."

Emily frowned. "What about it? Is Frank finished?"

"Emily, you need to call him now. I'm not very good at explaining financial things, and he can do a better job of it."

The phone crackled a bit. "Mom, I can't hear you very well."

"Honey, I think I'm losing the connection, but I want you to contact Frank!"

After ending the phone call with her mother, she called Frank. His deep voice carried over the wire. "Hi, Emily."

Her heart skipped a beat as she spoke. She told him about the birth of Becky's baby. "Mom's already left. She told me that I needed to call you about the audit."

"Can I come by tomorrow night?"

"Can you come by before that?"

"I wish I could, but I've got to finish up some stuff for my boss tonight. I promise I'll be there tomorrow."

Emily ended the call, wondering why Laura sounded so stressed.

ès

Frank entered his car, leaning his head back onto the headrest. After meeting with the alcoholic support group and speaking with Devon, he'd hoped he could stop drinking. When he was at his apartment the previous night, he'd thought he could have just a little bit to drink, just enough to take the edge off his raw pain. But once he'd sipped the alcohol, he couldn't stop himself, and he fell asleep sloshed.

He called Devon this morning, telling him what had happened the night before. Devon had again stressed his group was a Christian support group and in order for Frank to give up the alcohol completely, he would need to surrender himself to Jesus. "That's the only way you can find the strength to quit."

He wondered how he could surrender his life to someone. He wanted to deal with things his way and live his life according to his own rules.

He drove to Emily's, pushing the thoughts from his mind. He slowed his car and parked in the driveway once he'd reached the farm. Frank got out of the car and walked toward the barn, smelling the odor of animals and hay. He watched the black-and-white Holstein cows lined up in their stalls. Emily and a lanky teenager, whom he assumed was Jeremy or Darren, walked between the cows, milking four at a time. They worked together easily, and as the milk flowed through the pipes, the machines made a steady rhythm in the early evening heat.

Emily glanced up and smiled. "Frank! You're a little early!"

She didn't seem to be too upset, and he didn't want to interrupt her milking routine. He gestured toward the bovines. "I don't want to interrupt you. I'll talk to you when you're finished."

He watched her, drinking in her presence like an ice-cold glass of lemonade on a hot day. The joy that radiated from her face was like a ray of sunshine.

Since the milking was done, she sent the teen to feed the cows before she rinsed her milking equipment in the adjoining room. He stood beside her at the sink as she performed the chore.

He touched her shoulder. "Are you ready to talk right now?" he asked, touching the tendrils of her hair that escaped from her ponytail.

"Yes, we can talk now. What's happened with the audit for my farm? Mom sounded worried."

He sighed before he repeated the information he'd relayed to Laura the previous day. Emily's mouth dropped open, and her eyes widened. She backed away, shaking her head. "I don't believe you."

"I wish it wasn't true."

She stormed toward the teenager and told him to finish cleaning the milking equipment after he was finished feeding the cows and the bull. Frank followed her as she walked back to the house. "So, you're telling me that my father was a dishonest gambler?" She covered her quivering mouth. "That's not true! There's no way my father would place our farm in jeopardy."

Frank remained silent as she plopped onto the porch swing, unsure of how to comfort her.

She turned toward him, glaring. "So you're telling me that I could lose my farm, too?" Her large eyes filled with tears. "Is that what you're telling me?"

He ran his fingers over his head. "Yes, but—"

She looked away. "Are you sure you know what you're doing?"

The cold, hard edge to her voice frightened him. "What do you mean?"

"Were you sober the whole time you were auditing my farm?"

He clamped his mouth shut, shocked she would make such an implication. Taking a deep breath, he stood and walked away, unsure if she was serious or if she just needed an excuse because she didn't want to believe the truth about her father.

❧

Emily watched Frank return to his car, and her heart pulsed

with anger. She almost called him back, shocked at the words that had tumbled from her mouth. Shaking her head, she turned away from the accountant, staring at the corn and silos in the distance.

She wiped her tears away, her head suddenly aching. Rocking the swing in the warm breeze, she tried to digest Frank's bad news. She jumped when Darren stepped onto the porch. "Sorry, didn't mean to scare you." The teen gazed at her, his dark eyes full of curiosity. "Hey, are you okay, Miss Emily?"

She sniffed. "There's so much going on right now." When he made no attempt to leave, she asked, "Did you need something?"

He nodded, his short braids swinging. "Yes, it's payday. Remember?"

"Oh, yes." Once she had given him his pay and he'd left, she sat back on the porch.

Kelly pulled into the driveway and sauntered onto the porch when it started to get dark, still wearing her business suit and high heels. She plopped onto the swing beside Emily. "I was on my way home from work, and I thought I'd stop by." She peered into Emily's face. "What's wrong?"

Emily stared at the porch ceiling. "I can't even talk about it."

"You look zonked." She grabbed Emily's hand. "Come on inside."

Kelly fixed some peppermint tea and placed a plate of lemon cookies on the table. "Have something to drink or eat. You look awful."

Emily's stomach roiled, and she pushed the tea away.

"Em, drink the tea. Maybe it will help calm you down." After taking several deep breaths, she sipped the tea as Kelly sat at the table with her. "Now, tell me what's wrong."

"Frank said some terrible things about my father." Her voice sounded hoarse.

"What did he say?"

Emily could barely speak as she told her friend about Frank's accusations against her dad.

"Have you called Laura?"

"No, not yet. My mom did call me this morning, but I was out milking the cows. She left a message and said Becky and the baby are doing fine." She blew air through her lips. "I just don't know what to do. I don't know what to believe. And do you know what the worst part of it is?"

"What's that?"

She told her how she asked Frank if he was sober the entire time he was doing the audit.

Kelly gasped, and Emily moaned. "Em, I can't believe you said that."

"Frank looked so hurt when I said it."

"Maybe you should apologize to him," Kelly suggested.

"I probably should. I just got so mad when he said those things. I was angry, and I said the first thing that came to my mind."

"Did you know he's been attending Devon Crandall's alcoholic support group?"

Emily stared at her friend. "I told him to talk to Devon, and he told me he'd tried to go to a meeting but he chickened out."

"Well, I heard through the church grapevine that he's been attending. Maybe he's trying to give up the alcohol, Em."

Emily's mouth quivered. "Oh no. What if my insensitive comment makes him go home and drink?" She closed her eyes. "Kelly, I feel so bad. I just. . ."

Kelly rushed over to her friend. "Give him some time to cool off. I'm sure he knew you didn't mean it."

Emily sniffed. "All those things he said about Daddy—I just can't believe them. I just can't."

Kelly left and returned with some pills. "I found that prescription you filled for your sleeping pills right after your father died. Here's two. Why don't you take them and get a good night's sleep?"

Emily accepted the pills and took them. She found she just couldn't talk any longer after Kelly had taken her exit and the medicine settled into her body. Her muscles relaxed, and she soon stumbled up the stairs to her bedroom. For the first time in her whole farming career, she fell asleep wearing the same clothes she wore to milk the cows.

&

Frank slammed the door to the accounting office building on Pratt Street. He stood on the corner, gazing at the buildings in the distance. Late evening tourists and shoppers walked by, their arms heavy with colorful store bags. He pulled off his tie, hating the managerial meeting that had occurred that day in the main office. His firm required all upper-level managers to wear business attire to these meetings, and he wasn't in the mood to wear his suit today. His boss had also called him into his office, informing him that he'd appeared irritable and cranky lately and he wondered if something was wrong. Frank couldn't admit that he needed a drink—badly. Emily's comment the previous evening had haunted him all night, and he had almost drunk some of his favorite scotch to dull the pain. He'd finally dumped the scotch down the toilet before tossing and turning most of the night.

Once he got into the car, he dropped his head back on the seat, groaning. "Oh, God, I feel so bad right now." He started his car and pulled out of the lot. Forty minutes later, he pulled into a parking space at Monkton Christian Church, feeling a desperate need to meet with the alcoholic support group. He gazed at his Bible, still sitting on the passenger side of the car. Questions about God, life, and salvation filled his mind like unwanted weeds in a garden.

After walking into the practically deserted building, he entered the meeting room for the support group. During the meeting, he spoke of Emily's comment the previous evening and about how it had filled him with shame.

"Why were you ashamed?" asked one of the female attendees.

"Even though I was sober the whole time I was doing the audit, I could see myself getting to the point where I could have been drinking during the day." He went on to say that since he'd started drinking after his wife died, he noticed the amount of alcohol he consumed nightly had increased. "I've been waking up with bad headaches; sometimes I vomit."

Once the rest of the attendees had sprinkled in their words of wisdom and told of their weekly trials, Devon invited everybody to stand and join hands as they closed with a prayer. When the meeting was over, Frank pulled Devon aside. "I wanted to talk to you about something," said Frank.

Devon invited him to return to his seat. "You look upset," Devon observed. His wise, kind eyes bored into Frank.

"My addiction is really starting to bother me."

"I know it is. You're feeling guilty right now. I can tell." Devon's voice softened. "You know what you need to do. You need to surrender yourself to God."

"But that's so hard to do! My wife surrendered her life to God, but now she's dead."

"Her body is dead, but her spirit lives on. She's with Jesus right now, and you need to stop focusing on earthly life so much." He looked at Frank for a few seconds. "You know, Frank, I never did tell you my testimony. There's so much about me that I haven't had the chance to tell you yet." He checked his watch. "Are you in a hurry to leave?"

Frank dreaded the return to his empty apartment where thoughts of drinking continued to consume him. "No, I'm in no hurry."

They sat back down, and Devon began his testimony. "I grew up in a home where alcohol flowed like water."

Frank frowned. "Do you mean both of your parents drank?"

Devon nodded. "My brother and I knew how wine and beer tasted before we even started kindergarten."

Frank gasped, shocked. "Your parents gave you booze?"

"No, they didn't give it to us directly. They were just irresponsible about how they left it around the house. My brother and I could get into the alcohol and drink it. We hated the taste but discovered we could water it down and drink it. It made us feel grown up."

"Your parents never knew what you did?"

"Since both of my parents drank so frequently, they didn't realize what was happening. Steve—that's my brother—and I grew up thinking it was okay to drink and get sloshed. Although our father was an alcoholic, he was always quoting scripture, saying Jesus died for our sins and that it was okay that he was getting drunk every night because God had already forgiven him for that. Steve and I grew up with the philosophy that we could do what we wanted as far as drinking was concerned because it was what we'd been hearing all our lives."

"So what changed your mind?" Frank asked.

"Steve and I were in the car with our father, and he was very drunk. He almost fell asleep at the wheel, and the car swerved into a ditch." He looked at the wall for a few seconds. "None of us were hurt, but at that point, I could see my dad's philosophy about being drunk was skewed. However, I was almost sixteen, and I was used to drinking whenever I wanted."

"Did your father continue drinking after the accident?"

"Not right away. He sobered up for a month or so, but before long, he was hitting the bottle as hard as ever. My mother's drinking was just as bad, and as I got ready to graduate from high school, I found that I wasn't happy unless I was drinking. From the type of household I was raised in, I thought the way I felt and handled things was normal. What really made me change my life was when my brother died from a drunk driving accident." He wiped his eyes. "Losing my brother was the hardest thing I'd ever been through, and his death spurred me to look at myself emotionally and spiritually."

"What did you do?" asked Frank.

"Although I'd been raised by a father who quoted scripture all the time, I realized that I'd never really studied the Bible for myself, word for word, to see what God really said we should do to live a life that was pleasing to Him. I was twenty years old at the time, and I searched around until I found a small church where I felt comfortable. I began studying the scriptures with other believers until I finally proclaimed Christ as my Savior. My father died of liver disease because of his heavy drinking when I was twenty-five, but he'd learned to control his drinking after Steve died. My mom, dad, and I all found the Lord after Steve's death, and I make sure when I convince people to accept Christ that they hear about what I went through as I searched for the Lord."

Devon's testimony sank deeply into Frank's heart, and he still thought about Devon Crandall's words as he drove home that night.

ten

The following Saturday, Frank opened his eyes, blinking and feeling lousy. He swallowed, thinking about his tormented night. Emily's accusation still felt like a punch in the gut. He'd actually made it through the day without a drink, and he'd been on the phone with Devon last night for a whole hour. The urge for a drink consumed him, and he shuffled over to the coffee pot, making a large pot of the steaming brew. He sipped the coffee, recalling Devon's advice. "Son, you need to accept the Lord. Fall down on your knees and accept Him. Surrender your life to Him. That's the only way you can give up the drink."

The ringing telephone interrupted his musings, and he jumped. Groaning, he picked up the receiver. "Hello."

"Frank? It's Emily." Her smooth, sweet voice reminded him of silk. He relished the pleasure of hearing her speak.

"Emily? I'm surprised you called."

"I wanted to apologize for what happened the other day. I shouldn't have said those things to you."

He tried to think of the right words to say. The hurt from her accusation had pierced through him like a lightning bolt; still, he knew she was justified in her assumption, even though it was wrong. Finally, he spoke. "I. . .can I see you sometime today? I wanted to talk to you about something."

"You haven't had anything to drink today, have you? I don't want you to drive over here if you've been drinking. I know you're trying to quit. . ."

"It's hard to stop completely."

She sighed. "That's what I've heard. That's why I want to

make sure you're okay. I just don't want you driving over here if you're drinking. I worry about you, Frank."

"You don't have to worry about me. Remember I told you that I only drink at night after I get home," he reminded her.

They agreed to meet for dinner, and Emily offered to meet Frank in Baltimore, but he refused, telling her that he would pick her up.

❧

Darren showed up for work that evening, so after they milked the cows and fed them, she strolled toward the house as the conversation she'd had with Frank that morning still played in her mind. After removing her barn boots, she entered her home and went upstairs to take a long, hot shower, still contemplating the fate of her farm. After showering, she sprayed perfume over her skin before pulling her hair back into a ponytail. Sporting faded jeans and a large red T-shirt, she was more than ready to meet with Frank to discuss her farm.

The crunch of gravel signaled the approach of Frank's car. Emily bounded down the stairs and exited the house into the humid night. The sun was just beginning to set, and the sky was pink and bright orange. Her heart skipped a beat when he touched her arm.

"It's nice to see you again," he said.

She nodded. "It's good to see you, too."

They were soon in his Lexus, taking the forty-minute drive toward downtown Baltimore. While driving, he told her about his recent conversations with Mark and how Trish still worried about the boy's erratic behavior. "I just wish his father would take a more active role in his life," he said. Emily was touched that Frank was so worried about his nephew. He spoke about it so frequently that he almost seemed like a father instead of an uncle.

"Do you mind if we go to the M & S Grill?" he asked when they arrived in Baltimore.

"I don't mind."

They entered the spacious restaurant, and she wondered why Frank had brought his briefcase with him. Their server approached. "We'd like an outside table," Frank informed her.

They ordered sodas when they were seated, and before the server could leave, Frank asked Emily a question. "Do you mind if I order for both of us?"

Food was the last thing on her mind. "I don't mind."

He ordered the flounder stuffed with crab imperial for both of them. "I've been doing a lot of eating out since I've been here. They make the best stuffed flounder."

His leg jiggled, and she touched his hand. "Are you okay?"

He sighed, looking toward the water. Boats bobbed in the hot breeze, and if there weren't so many issues between them, Emily could imagine having a pleasant time with Frank this evening.

His dark, mesmerizing eyes looked tortured. "No, I'm not okay. I need a drink."

She took a deep breath before voicing her next question. "Have you stopped drinking?"

"Sort of."

She frowned, still touching his hand. "What do you mean?" He told her how he'd stopped but then gotten intoxicated a few nights ago.

"Have you had a drink since?"

"No."

"Well, that's good then. You're on the right track." She tried to remain positive. Groups of teenagers strolled down the sidewalk, laughing as they passed on the busy pavement. "Has Devon Crandall been helping you?"

"Yes, I've been speaking to Devon over the last few weeks. He's a nice guy. He's caring."

"Yes, Devon's been through a lot. Did he share his testimony with you?"

"Yes, but he says I need to accept Christ if I want to find the strength to quit drinking completely."

"He's right. You've got to give God a chance." He ran his fingers over his short hair. "I know what your problem is." He remained silent. "You just like having complete control over your life."

Shock etched his face. "Yeah, so what?"

She shook her head. "But you're not controlling your life. The alcohol is." He winced, looking away. She squeezed his hand. "Frank, you can't control your life. You've got to let God help you."

They silently sipped their drinks for a few seconds before she gestured toward his briefcase. "Why did you bring that?"

Sighing, he removed a thick stack of cream-colored paper. "Emily, here's what I wanted to discuss with you."

He went through former tax returns and worksheets, explaining things to Emily. "Bottom line, you owe the IRS this amount of money." He pointed to a large figure on the paper.

Emily gasped. Their flounder arrived, but she had lost her appetite. The server left their food at the side of the table since they were still looking through Frank's papers. "Does this mean that if Laura and I don't pay this back, we'll lose the farm?"

Frank slowly nodded. "You could lose your farm." He quickly squeezed her hand. "But, there are ways to get around this that might work."

Emily blinked, still trying to drink in all the information. "Like what?"

He opened his napkin, avoiding her intense gaze. "I've already contacted the IRS—"

Her mouth dropped open. "You already reported my father?"

Grabbing her hand, he rubbed her palm, and her anger

disappeared like a calm sea after a raging storm. "You know I wouldn't report your father to the IRS without clearing it with you or Laura first." He sighed, still holding her hand. "I just contacted them, without giving any personal information, and asked how I could advise a client about their situation. I didn't give the name of you or your family." He looked at her directly. "You could possibly get a bank loan, but I doubt it since your father already has that farm mortgaged to the brim."

Emily continued to stare at Frank. "Do you have any other suggestions?"

Frank released her hand. Without answering her question, he pulled their plates from the side of the table, placing one in front of Emily and one in front of himself. He took a large bite of his flounder. She wondered how he could eat at a time like this and why he wouldn't answer her question.

She looked at her plate. The delicate white fish made her stomach churn. Taking her fork, she took a small bite.

Frank sipped his Coke. "Emily, I don't know how you feel about this."

"About what?" She put her fork aside, giving him her full attention.

"Well, I could give you the resources so your farm won't be confiscated."

She gasped. "I can't accept that kind of money from you."

He took another sip of Coke. "It could be a loan."

Gritting her teeth, she gazed toward the Chesapeake Bay. "I don't know if we could pay you back."

"Don't worry about that yet. I just want to do what I can so that you won't lose your farm." She stared at his bent head as he ate.

"Why would you do this for me?"

He didn't respond, and she wondered why he refused to look at her.

"Frank?" She placed her hand over his arm, forcing him to stop eating his meal.

"I. . .I just want to do this."

She looked at the patrons at the surrounding tables eating their evening meals, still trying to comprehend. "But I still don't understand. . ."

"I just want to help out a friend. What's wrong with that?"

She gazed at him, still trying to decipher his actions. She was unsure of what to say. Her deep feelings for Frank rushed through her, but she knew that if she was indebted to him, it would make their situation sticky. She pushed the papers toward him. "I can't talk about this anymore."

❧

Once Frank dropped her off, Emily's mind was spinning. She'd called Laura, but she was in the midst of serving dinner to Becky's family, and there was chaos in the background. "Mom, call me back later tonight when you get a chance. It's okay if you wake me up." Since there was a three-hour time difference, Emily didn't want Laura to hesitate about calling her if she thought she was going to wake her.

She sat on the couch in the dark living room and didn't realize she'd fallen asleep until the phone awakened her. She lifted the receiver. "Hello."

"Hey, Emily. It's Kelly."

"And Christine. Kelly has us on three-way."

"Hi, guys." Emily cleared her throat, still trying to clear her sleep-clogged brain.

"You sound like you're asleep," said Christine.

"Why are you all calling me on three-way?"

Christine responded, "Kelly wanted to tell us about her date."

"Emily, Antoine is the greatest!" said Kelly.

"He is?" asked Emily.

"Yeah, and you know I only met him a few weeks ago."

Emily nodded. "I remember you mentioning that. You said he's a new member of the choir."

"Well, he picked me up and gave me flowers!" She giggled. "And he took me to that fancy restaurant downtown!" She continued to gush about her date, not giving them a chance to respond. "He's so cute! He's got those light brown eyes and full lips that were made for kissing! We talked constantly through the meal, and when he dropped me off, he kissed my cheek, and he wanted to know when we could see each other again!"

Emily smiled. "I can tell you want to see him again."

Christine interjected. "You know she does. That's why she's calling us on three-way—so she can tell both of us about this wonderful man!"

"You guys, of course I want to see him again! Emily, it's been such a long time since I've dated anybody! I don't count Martin as dating since I only saw him twice."

"What happened with Martin, anyway? You never did tell us," said Emily.

Kelly groaned. "Well, I don't want to spoil a good evening talking about Martin."

Christine spoke. "Well, you should at least tell us what happened. You used to talk about him all the time, and then when you stopped seeing him, you wouldn't tell us why."

Kelly was silent for a few seconds before she spoke. "Well, when I was talking to Martin, we were talking about Christianity and faith. He blatantly asked me about, well, you know, having sex with him even though I was a Christian. He said that he was a Christian and his belief in God didn't stop him from doing what he wanted. That's when I decided I couldn't see him again. He said that I wasn't open-minded enough to date him, so that was the end of that."

All three women were silent for a few seconds before Emily spoke. "Well, you did the right thing, Kelly."

Christine sighed. "I'm beginning to wonder if any eligible men exist around here."

Kelly stated her opinion. "You never know. I guess we should just trust God and not worry about this so much."

Christine spoke. "Emily, what's been going on with you?"

Emily stood. "Hold on, my throat is dry. Let me get a glass of water." After filling a glass, she guzzled the cold liquid down, relieving her parched throat. When she sat back down, she told Kelly and Christine about her conversation with Frank.

"He offered you that money because he loves you!" said Kelly.

Emily wondered if Kelly was telling the truth. "Loves me? Frank doesn't love me. He's never told me this."

Christine interjected. "I haven't had a serious relationship in years, but from my limited experience, love is very complicated."

Emily clutched the receiver. "How do you guys know Frank loves me?"

Kelly sighed. "You should see the way he stares at you in church! He loves you, girl. I don't know why he hasn't told you yet, but I'm sure he'll tell you eventually."

"I don't think he loves me."

"Yes, he loves you, Emily," Christine said. "Now stop being so hardheaded about it and accept it for what it is."

They talked for a few more minutes before finally saying good night. But her friends' words rang in her ears as she trudged up the stairs to get ready for bed.

੨੪

Frank struggled through life the next few weeks. The urge to drink washed through him in waves, and he spoke to Devon daily. The older man had advised him to take it one day at a time. "That way your whole situation won't seem so hopeless," he'd said.

Emily filtered through his mind constantly, and he still wanted her to accept his offer of help for her farm. When his boss had called him into his office again, he'd reminded Frank that his temporary venture to start up the farm and ranch accounting division of their company had come to an end. "You've done an awesome job, and you've worked a tremendous amount of overtime. Would you like to stay as part of the farm and ranch division here in Baltimore, or would you rather return to Chicago? The choice is yours."

He walked along the grounds of the Cylburn Arboretum in Baltimore City, his boss's words running through his mind like a speeding train. Since Frank had agreed that it was best he return to Chicago, his boss had hired a replacement for him. The company event at the Arboretum was a threefold celebration: Frank's going-away celebration, the new hire's welcome party, and a celebration of the success of their new division.

His company had rented a room on the first floor of the building, and when his coworkers drank glasses of champagne, Frank thought he would lose his mind. He'd frowned when the alcoholic beverage was popped open by a catering employee. As the beige-colored liquid was poured into glass flutes, his boss must have noted his reaction when he'd approached him. "Don't frown so much, Franklin. We're off the clock now, so we can have a drink to celebrate our success. We do the same thing when we have our Christmas party every year."

Frank had nodded, heat rushing through him. His boss had placed his hand on Frank's arm. "You look like you could use a drink. Let me get you a glass."

Frank had shaken his head. "No. I'm not feeling too good right now. I think I'll go for a walk on the grounds." He'd practically fled the large mansion and onto the landscaped property. The warm sun soothed him as he walked farther away from the building. He finally found a bench outside in the massive garden. Colorful butterflies fluttered above the large expanse of flowers. The rainbow of blooms created a carpet of color, surrounding him with their scent. The leaves on the nearby trees were turning color, hinting at the autumn weather that was coming soon. "Lord, what am I going to do?"

He continued to take pleasure in his surroundings as thoughts filtered through his brain. He recalled Devon's advice. "Give the Lord a chance, son. That's about all you can do to keep the alcohol away." Emily's sweet face came to mind, and he recalled her words of wisdom as they'd shared dinner together. "Frank, you can't control your life. You've got to let God help you."

He recalled Julie's happiness once she'd accepted Jesus into her life. Tears stained his cheeks as a black and yellow butterfly hovered around his bench. He wiped his eyes, realizing he couldn't control his life on his own anymore. He needed help—in the worst way. "Lord, help me. I'm a sinner; please help me, Lord." His shoulders shook as he cried and accepted God's grace for his sins.

❧

A few days later when Emily returned home from running errands, she was shocked to see Frank's Lexus parked in her driveway. He'd been to church the last couple of Sundays but had rushed off before she had a chance to speak with him. Her farm's fate weighed upon her mind, and she realized that once Laura returned, they would need to sit down and decide what to do about the back taxes owed on their property.

She exited her truck, holding several bags of purchases. Frank sat on her screened-in porch, waiting for her. His trusty leather briefcase stood upright on the floor, and she wondered why he had brought it with him. They gazed at each other, silent.

"Hi," he finally greeted.

The bags grew heavy in her arms, and she almost dropped

them before Frank came to her rescue. "Here, let me help you with those."

"Thanks," she mumbled. They carried the bags into the house and placed them on the table.

He touched her shoulder. "You look tired. Are you okay?"

"It's been a rough day."

"Did something happen?"

She dropped her purse on the table. "Yes, the inspector showed up this morning." Emily explained how the inspector would show up unannounced periodically, making sure their dairy farm fit the government's standards.

"Did he find anything wrong?"

"No, but he sure tried. He was here long enough, poking around. I just wanted him to leave."

"Did anything else happen?"

"Thunderbolt got out."

"Huh?"

"Thunderbolt is one of the cows. She's feisty and fast. She's new to the milking herd, and when Jeremy and I were letting the cows out to graze this morning, Thunderbolt ran right past us." She pouted. "It was awful. We ran into the street to get her back. It took us a whole hour to coax her back to the farm, and she held up traffic."

He glanced around the silent house. "Is Laura here?" he asked.

She placed a carton of milk in the refrigerator. "No, she's still in California."

"When will she be back?"

Emily sat, suddenly too weary to put the rest of the groceries away. "She'll be back next week. She has to start working at the cafeteria again because school's already started. She called the school, and they said she could start a couple of weeks late. The C-section is about healed, and Becky's getting used to the baby's constant demands." She talked about her stepsister's plight for a few minutes before she realized she was babbling. "I know you didn't come here to get an update on Becky's health."

"No, I didn't." Sunlight streamed into the bright, airy kitchen, highlighting Frank's pleasant features. Emily realized she could just sit and stare at this man forever. She pushed the thought from her mind, realizing there was little hope for them to have a relationship. He lifted his briefcase, placing it on the table. Snapping the gold locks open, he removed a sheaf of papers. "You never took the final paperwork for the audit of your farm." He placed the cream-colored papers on the table.

"Thanks."

"As soon as I leave, I want you to promise me you'll look through all this."

She gestured toward the papers. "I'll get to it eventually."

He shook his head. "Please promise me you'll at least glance through them after I've left."

His dark eyes were full of sadness when he gazed at her, and she wondered if everything was okay. "I promise." When silence weighed heavily in the kitchen again, she spoke. "You just came to bring me the papers?"

He sighed when he sat. He ran his fingers over his short dark hair, and the familiar gesture warmed her heart. "No, that's not the only reason I came." He paused. "I'm going back to Chicago."

Her heart stopped. "You're kidding."

"I wouldn't kid about this, sweetheart."

"But. . .but why?"

"I told you that I was initially here for a temporary time."

"You can't stay?" she mumbled.

He shook his head. "I'd like to but. . ." He balled his hands into fists. "I have to make things right with my folks." He took a deep breath. "I don't think I have much time left, so I have to go home."

"Did something happen with you parents?"

"Trish called me a few hours ago. My dad's had a stroke."

"Oh no! Will he be okay?"

"No, the doctors don't expect him to live long. I have to go home."

She patted his shoulder. "Of course you do. I'll be praying for you and your family." So many questions littered her brain like unwanted weeds in a garden. Would Frank be coming back? Would this be the last time she'd see him? Would he ever accept Christ?

"I don't know when I'll be strong enough to come back."

She took his hand. "Frank, please give God a chance. Just come to Him as you are, and He'll accept you. He'll give you the strength to get you through anything. You don't have to fix yourself before you come to Jesus."

"I've given up alcohol for a short time, and it's been terrible." He told her about his experience at the Cylburn Arboretum. "Emily, I'm a sinner in the worst way. Even before my father had a stroke, I was still planning on going to Chicago."

His words surprised her, and she realized they could find a way to make it work between them with the Lord's help. "Frank, we're all sinners. Although you say you've accepted Christ, it sounds like you're still harboring guilt. Jesus doesn't want us to feel guilty. Let Him take all that guilt and sadness off your shoulders. Jesus has already paid the price for all our sins. If you follow the Lord, that'll give you the strength you need."

"I'm a new Christian, and I'm still trying to make my life right. I don't know how long I can stay away from alcohol, even with the Lord on my side." With his father's predicament, he knew he'd find it hard not to drink. "It's unfair of me to want to be with you, knowing I'm so weak."

His words made her speechless. She stared at him, drinking him in, not knowing what to say or do. Soon he was beside her, and his lips touched hers in a brief, tender kiss. She didn't realize she was crying until Frank gave her a napkin from the dispenser on the table. "Are you coming back?" she asked softly.

"I don't know. I'd like to come back when I feel I'm no longer a threat."

"What do you mean?"

"I'm an alcoholic. You've never seen me when I'm drunk. It's not pleasant. It's not right for me to be with you if I turn back to the bottle again."

"We could try. With the Lord's help, we can make it work."

"I have faith, but I don't think my faith is as strong as yours. I'm still praying about it, asking the Lord to lead me into doing the right things. I know He wants me to return to Chicago and spend some time with my dad since I don't know how long he will live." He glanced away for a few seconds. "My mother's always depended on my dad, and I think it'll break her if he dies." He looked at his watch. "I have to get going."

"So you're driving back?"

"Yes, I had a moving company come and take my stuff to Trish's house. She lives in a large home outside of Chicago, and I'll be staying with her until I've made other living arrangements. The movers left this morning, and Trish is expecting them."

"Can we at least keep in touch? I'd like to know how your father is doing." She also wanted to know how Frank was doing.

"Yes, I'd like that."

She wanted to know if he wanted her to wait for him, but she couldn't bring herself to voice those words. He gestured toward the papers before removing his car keys from the pocket of his jeans. "Be sure to keep your promise to me and read those papers after I leave?"

She nodded, still speechless. The screen door banged shut

when he left, and gravel crunched beneath his tires as he drove away from the farm.

She watched Frank's burgundy Lexus until it disappeared from view. She then took the stack of papers he'd left and sat on the porch.

The letter was from Franklin Reese, CPA, stating the validity of the financial papers and the results of his audit. Emily didn't understand most of the terms and language, but she recognized a lot of the stuff Frank had shown her at the restaurant the other day. The papers outlined the violations her father had committed and recommended going to the IRS with a payment plan to repay the back taxes. He'd also placed a side note, stating that his replacement, Melvin Sparks, could be entrusted to contact the IRS on their behalf and with filing the amended returns. If they repaid the money, he doubted there would be a lot of trouble from the government agency.

There was also a bill enclosed, noting Frank's hours, but the bill was marked PAID IN FULL. Emily fingered the cream-colored stationery, shocked that they did not have to pay for Frank's labor.

Frank had also enclosed a check for enough money to cover the balance due to the IRS. She hugged the envelope to her chest. "Oh, Daddy, why did you have to die? Why did you have to be so dishonest?" She sniffed, crying tears of grief. *Lord, what am I supposed to do now? Daddy's dead, Frank is gone, and Laura won't be back for a while. I feel so lost and alone, Lord. Please help me find some peace.*

After much prayer, thought, and deliberation, Emily decided to accept Frank's gift. The day she deposited the funds, she fell on her knees, saying a prayer to God.

eleven

As the months passed following Frank's departure, Emily found that her thoughts of Frank continued to haunt her. He e-mailed her a few times, and she knew his father had eventually died. She'd wanted to call him, but she wasn't sure if he wanted to speak with her. She moped about the house, did farm chores, and helped their hired workers harvest the corn. Kelly and Christine came over often, and they called periodically, but her friends couldn't cheer her up. One day after church in November, Emily and her stepmother went downtown for a lazy afternoon. They stopped at the Baltimore Cupcake Company for a snack. Both of them chose chocolate truffle cupcakes with beautiful floral-patterned icing to go with their cups of Café du Monde.

They sat at a table, and the brilliant sunlight spilled into the space as they ate their treat. When Emily finished her cupcake, she was almost tempted to lick the stray icing from her fingers. "I wish I could have another one."

Laura gave her a mischievous grin. "Why don't we get another?"

"Mom!" Emily patted her hips. "I don't need the extra calories."

"Don't worry about it. You're so thin, and you're always out there doing farm chores. I don't think you have anything to worry about." Feeling naughty, Emily complied and returned to the counter, purchasing them vanilla truffle cupcakes. Once they had finished their second round of cupcakes, Emily sipped her coffee. "Are you glad to be back in Monkton?" she asked Laura.

Laura shrugged. "I miss your father. But it is nice to be back and into a routine again. I like working at the school cafeteria and seeing the kids every day." A wistful look crossed her face as she stirred her coffee.

"Mom, what's wrong? You've been acting like something's been on your mind since you returned from Becky's."

Laura shrugged. "It's nothing I feel like talking about right now."

Emily tasted another bite of cupcake, figuring Laura would tell her what was on her mind when she was ready. She gazed at the street, thinking about Frank and the last words they'd exchanged before he left for Chicago.

"You're thinking of Frank, aren't you?" asked her stepmother, sipping her coffee.

Emily placed her cup on the table. "How did you know?"

"I can always tell when you're thinking about him." They sat in silence for a few moments, watching the cars pass by on the street.

"I was just thinking about how I got to know him while he was here." She told Laura about the close bond he shared with his nephew and about how he used to mentor teens at the rec center in Chicago. Emily thought he'd make a great father but didn't want to voice that opinion. If she dwelled on that too much, it would just make her long for something that might never happen.

"You know, you've been through a lot lately."

Emily shrugged, sipping her hot drink. "I guess so."

"I have a suggestion to make."

"What's that?"

"I wondered if you wanted to go and visit your cousin Monica in Ocean City for a week."

"But what about the farm?"

"I've already spoken to some people, and we have enough extra help so that you can go on a vacation. You need it. When

I was in Florida following Paul's death, it did wonders for my mental health."

"I don't know." She kind of found some solace just spending time with the animals each day.

Her stepmother touched her hand. "You've been moody lately, and I know Frank really hurt your feelings when he left. I think a change in scenery may help you out of your mood."

When Emily finished her coffee, she told Laura she would call and check with Monica. If she said it was okay, she'd take her vacation the following week. Maybe the change in scenery was what she needed.

❧

The following week, Emily arrived at her cousin's house. Monica and her husband, John, welcomed her into their home. She also got a chance to visit with Monica's sister, Gina, and Scotty, Gina's blind nine-year-old son. The child read a lot of braille books and magazines, and Monica confided how Scotty's educational needs were what brought her together with John. She'd explained that John was Scotty's tutor, and that was how they'd met.

One day, following a fun-filled Saturday of sightseeing in Ocean City, they returned to Monica's house for dinner. "I'm going to start the oven," said John, kissing Monica's cheek before heading into the kitchen. He was making lasagna for their meal while Monica visited with Emily in the living room.

"John is very affectionate toward you," Emily commented.

Monica chuckled. "Yes, he is. I just never thought I'd fall so deeply in love."

"I'm sorry I missed your wedding last year. Dad had the flu, and I had to stay and take care of the farm."

Monica smiled. "That's okay." She stood and walked to the other side of the room, opening an oak cabinet and removing a large leather book. "Here are our wedding pictures."

Emily admired the photos. "These are beautiful."

"Thanks." Once she had looked at all the pictures, Monica told Emily some news. "I'm pregnant."

Emily's heart filled with joy. "You're kidding."

"Nope! We can hardly wait."

She hugged her cousin. "I'm so happy for both of you; I really am." When they broke their embrace, tears slipped from Emily's eyes, and Monica handed her a tissue.

She touched Emily's shoulder. "Cousin, why are you so sad?"

Emily wondered if Monica would truly understand her problems, but she had to tell Monica all that had happened since her father's death. "I just can't believe my father was a gambler." She told her about Frank, his drinking, his salvation, and his sudden disappearance from her life. "He's e-mailed me a few times, but I miss him like crazy."

"Why do you like him so much?" Monica asked.

"He's kind, he's caring, he's conscientious, and I like being with him. I like being around him. I hated his drinking, and the fact that he was unsaved really bothered me. Now that he's saved, I'd hoped we could work things out. But it looks like I was wrong. I just wish he wasn't afraid of turning into an alcoholic again, but I can't make his desire to drink go away."

"Does he still talk to you? Other than the e-mails?"

"He doesn't call me, but he is in Chicago right now, and I know his father died. We don't have constant contact, just an occasional e-mail."

"Have you thought about calling him?"

"No. I sense he doesn't want to talk to me." Another thought occurred to her. "You know, maybe he doesn't like me very much."

"He offered to save your farm for you. I think he likes you a lot, but he's working through his issues right now."

She shook her head. "No. There's no hope for us."

"Girl, where's your faith? If the Lord allowed John and me to be together, then I know there's hope for you and Frank."

"What do you mean?"

Monica gazed at the photo album. "John was an agnostic."

"Really? I didn't know that."

"Yeah. He didn't even know if he believed God existed. When he first started tutoring my nephew, we shared an instant attraction, but I knew there was no hope for us because of his beliefs."

"But he accepted Jesus," Emily guessed.

"He sure did. So, since God saw fit to bring John and I together, then He might see fit to bring you together with Frank."

"I just wish I could get Frank off my mind."

"Are you involved in any of the ministries at your church?" Emily told her about the outreach ministry. "Is there a singles group at your church?"

"There's one that just started shortly after Frank left. Kelly, Christine, and I joined, but I just haven't felt like going to the meetings. Why do you ask?"

"It might be more fun and fulfilling to hang out with other Christian singles. I remember when I was in the singles group at my church a long time ago, I never met anybody to date, but I had a good time. We'd have fun and fellowship time, and we'd go bowling, out to dinner, out to the movies." Monica shrugged. "It was fun, and it gave me something to do. Also, what do you like to do in your spare time besides work on your dairy farm?"

"Years ago I used to read novels, but it's something I just stopped doing."

"Well, why don't you start doing that again? If I recall, during the winter you don't have as much to do on your farm as you do during the summer months since you're not harvesting any crops or baling hay. If you're worried about spending a lot of money on books, you could always go to the library or a used book store."

"So you're saying that I need to keep myself busy and not worry about Frank so much?"

"Exactly. I certainly can't predict if he'll come back, but if it's the Lord's will, then Frank will come sweeping back to Monkton to be with you again. But if he doesn't come back, at least you'll be so occupied with your new activities that you'll barely notice. When I was pining after a man, another thing I did was get more acquainted with God. Why don't you try reading some more of the Word and focusing on God? I know it'd help."

"You make it sound so easy."

Monica touched Emily's shoulder. "By no means is it easy. I'm not saying doing all these things will make Frank disappear from your mind, but it might help. I can honestly say that I know how you feel, but you just have to take it one day at a time and try and focus on yourself and God until you find out what Frank's going to do."

Emily pondered Monica's words for the rest of the evening.

twelve

Four months later

"Would you like another soda?" Cameron Jacobs held Emily's hand, leading her to their seats at the spring gospel concert. People milled about, trying to find their seats in the arena as several waited near the stage, eager for the performance to start.

"I'm fine, Cameron." She put her cold soda aside, no longer thirsty.

Emily continued to think about Frank periodically and wondered why he had only e-mailed her briefly a few times. She still clung to Monica's hope that Frank would find help for his issues and return to Baltimore County; however, as time passed, her prayers remained unanswered, and she wondered if maybe the Lord was nudging her to let go of her fantasy of being with Frank.

During the holiday season a few months ago, she'd mailed him a Christmas card. She'd hoped and prayed for a response, but she had only received Frank's silence.

She gazed around the arena. The gospel concert was one of her favorite yearly events. This year, however, the festive music failed to lift her spirits. Sighing, she ran her fingers through her hair.

"I like your new haircut, Emily. It looks good on you."

Emily smiled her thanks to Cameron, although "new" wouldn't describe her haircut. A short time after her visit to Monica, she felt the weight of her long, dark hair to be too much to handle. She'd visited her hairdresser and asked for a short, snazzy cut.

The band warmed up, and Emily thought about the last four months of her life—about how she ended up coming to this gospel concert with Cameron.

Weeks following her visit with Monica, Cameron had asked her out yet again, so she finally relented and went out with the man. He was a person of strong faith, and she wondered if the Lord was trying to tell her that Cameron was the man she should pursue.

This was their fifth date, and so far Emily felt nothing for Cameron except feelings of friendship. He barely crossed her mind throughout her day, and he didn't haunt her dreams, unlike Frank.

"Emily!" Emily snapped out of her reverie, gazing at Cameron's confused expression. "The concert is over."

"Oh, sorry." She smiled and stood, gathering her coat. Cameron helped her with her garment, and she watched several other members of the audience retrieve their things as they headed to the large parking lot.

They drove home in silence. Emily gazed at the brightly lit windows of the stores downtown. Huddling into her coat, she was eager to return home and finish reading the Christian cozy mystery novel she'd started earlier that week. When Cameron pulled into the lot, she noticed another car in her driveway.

"Are you and your mother expecting company tonight?"

Emily frowned at the unfamiliar car. "I don't think so. But sometimes people from the church will drop by and visit." She remained silent when Cameron rushed out of the car and opened her door for her.

He walked her to the bottom of her porch. Emily sensed from the eager expression on Cameron's face that he was anticipating a good night kiss or an invitation inside for a piece of Laura's apple pie. She quickly bid him good night and turned away, not even giving him a chance to kiss her.

He stopped her with a question. "You don't like me very much, do you?"

She turned toward him again. "I think you're a nice man."

"Nice? You don't like me the way you liked that accountant that used to work out here. I saw the way you used to look at him in church."

Emily didn't want to hurt Cameron's feelings. "I think you're a strong, good man, and I admire your faith in God."

His shoulders drooped. "I won't ask you out anymore, Emily. I feel like I'm wasting my time."

She didn't want him to feel bad. "Cameron. Don't get mad."

"I'm not mad. It's just. . .whenever I'm with you, I feel like you're not with me."

She frowned, squinting at him in the darkness. "What do you mean?"

"Your mind is always on something. Half the time when I speak to you, I have to repeat myself. I almost get the feeling you can't wait for our dates to end."

Emily inwardly winced, hating that Cameron could read her so easily. "I'm sorry, Cameron." She held out her hand, not wanting things to end on a bad note. "We're still friends, right?"

He gave her a small smile, shaking her hand. "Yeah, we're still friends. I'll be seeing you when I come to get your milk tomorrow." He gestured toward the porch. "Since your house is dark and you don't recognize that car in your driveway, I'll just walk you to your door and make sure you get in okay."

"Thanks." His heavy footsteps followed her up the porch steps as she opened the creaky screen door. Cameron was right behind her as she tried to locate the door handle to the house in the darkness.

"Emily." A figure appeared, and Emily almost screamed when Cameron jumped on the person trespassing on their porch. Cameron and the trespasser landed on the floor, making a huge racket. "Get off me! Emily, it's me, Frank!"

"Oh my." Her voice trembled and her hands shook as she jerked the kitchen door open, turning on the light. The men stood simultaneously, Cameron glaring at Frank.

"You could have let Emily know you were on the porch instead of scaring her," Cameron said. "Emily, do you want me to stay, or are you okay alone with him?" Cameron shot a look at Frank.

"I'm fine, Cameron. Thanks for seeing me to my door." Cameron nodded, took his exit, and drove away, his taillights disappearing as he rounded the corner.

Her fright subsided when she entered the kitchen, and she quickly disarmed their recently installed burglar alarm before beckoning Frank inside. Her heart was pounding so hard, she felt it would pop out of her chest.

Suddenly, Frank was bathed in a warm glow, and Emily noticed the changes in him. He removed his leather jacket, and her breathing intensified when she looked up into his cocoa brown eyes. She gazed at his face, which now sprouted a thick beard and mustache.

"Frank, I. . . Why are you here?" Her voice shook, and she slowly sat at the kitchen table.

He shrugged, continuing to stare. "I came to see you. Laura wasn't home, so I decided to wait for you on the porch. Didn't you notice my car outside?"

Emily nodded. Her legs felt weightless as blood rushed to her head. "It's not the same car you had. . .you had when you left."

He chuckled. "That's right. I'd forgotten that you haven't seen my new car."

She shrugged. "When I saw your car, I just figured we had a visitor. I don't know where Laura is," she began before she spotted the note on the refrigerator. Emily read the note, which said that her stepmother was going to be spending the night with a troubled church member. "Laura won't be home tonight. She's been really busy since she joined the church's outreach program." She placed the note on the table.

"I don't recall Laura being in the outreach ministry before. I thought you were a part of that ministry."

She didn't feel like talking about church activities. But she forced herself to comment on Frank's observation. "I decided to stop being in that ministry, and my stepmother offered to take my place." She shrugged. "I had other ministries I wanted to be involved with." She pointed to the pile of books in the corner of the kitchen. "I've been reading some good Christian novels lately, and I've started a book club at my church. I've also been involved with the singles ministry, too. These things keep me busy. I still have a lot of chores to do on the farm, but not nearly as many as during the summertime."

When he began asking questions about her farm and her herd, Emily answered before she finally stopped herself, not wanting to act like things were okay between them. "Are you here visiting?" she asked abruptly.

"Emily, I'm back in Monkton for good now." Emily stared at Frank, wondering if this was another dream. "A lot has happened to me over the last six months."

She listened to him, still finding it hard to believe he was in her kitchen, talking as if they'd just seen each other yesterday. He ran his hand over his head, and the familiar gesture warmed her heart. "You know I was pretty messed up when I left."

"You mean with your drinking?"

He nodded. "You know I had a big problem with that. It was the only way I had to deal with Julie's death and my parents' decision not to accept her into the family."

"Have you stayed sober since you've been gone?"

"I haven't had a drink since that day I told you I'd stopped. But it's been a real struggle."

"Has it been more of a struggle since your father passed?"

"Yes. My father's death hit the family hard. It was so much to handle all at one time. My sister helped me out a lot with strengthening my faith."

"How are Trish's children? I'm assuming you spent a lot of time with them while you were in Chicago."

"Mark and Regina are fine. Trish and I are thankful that Mark hasn't gotten into any more trouble, but we still think he feels hurt because his father won't come to visit him very often."

"Did you find a nice church home in Chicago?"

"Yes. Although I have a church family in Chicago, I call Devon Crandall a lot since we've become friends. I also kept thinking about what you told me right before I returned to Chicago. You told me that I didn't need to fix myself before coming to Jesus, that He'd accept me as I am. I thought about that a lot over the last few months."

"I'm glad I said something that could help you. But did your father's death make you want to start drinking again?"

He stared at her with his beautiful brown eyes. "I was tempted to drink, yes. But I didn't. I had to pray to the Lord every day to make it through the day without having a drink." He opened his mouth as if he were going to say more, but he remained silent.

"Were you going to say something else?"

"No." Silence filled the kitchen, almost as if each of them had to digest the presence of the other.

Frank massaged her fingers, and she didn't have the strength to pull away. "I've missed you so much. You don't know how many times I've picked up the phone to call you but then decided against it."

She shrugged as feelings of joy and apprehension continued to course through her veins. "Why didn't you call? I wondered how you were doing. I sent you a Christmas card, and you never responded."

He sighed. "Because I had so many things to sort through and to work out in my life, I didn't want to call you before I'd set my life straight," he repeated.

"So everything is fine with you now?"

"Yes, it is. I asked if I could transfer back to the Monkton office, and they let me transfer."

"And now what are you going to do?"

"I'd like for us to date and get to know each other again."

Emily couldn't believe his words. "Date me?"

He sat up. "I'm a new man now. I'd like for you to get to know me better, and I'd like to spend some time with you again."

"I can't believe you did all this—relocated and everything—without calling me first. You could have warned me you were coming."

"I was sitting on the porch when you were talking to Cameron. I heard everything he said. I know you don't have feelings for him."

Emily inwardly winced, upset that Frank had heard such a private conversation. It was also highly upsetting that Cameron had mentioned Frank when they were talking. Before she could speak, Frank made another comment. "Are you dating somebody else besides Cameron?"

"I don't think that's any of your business." He dropped her hand, frowning. "I'm sorry. I shouldn't have said that."

"You're angry with me."

"I'm just. . .I'm just surprised to see you. You didn't even call me to tell me you were coming. You could have at least called and let me know you'd be here instead of sneaking on my porch and waiting for me."

He frowned. "I wasn't sneaking. It's not my fault that you were out on a date when I decided to come."

"You could have at least warned me that you'd be here."

"I felt the Lord leading me to come back here and live.

I should have called you, but I guess I just wasn't thinking clearly. I wanted to surprise you."

"Well, you did surprise me. I—"

"I love you." His voice was so low that she had to strain to hear it.

"What?"

"I said I love you, Emily. I know it's hard to believe, but I do. I've loved you for months, but I knew there was no hope between us until I straightened out my life." He scooted closer to her and kissed her palm.

She pulled her hand away. "I don't know if I'm ready for us to date, Frank."

Frank's face fell. "I understand. Will you at least think about going out with me tomorrow?" When she remained silent, he found pen and paper on the kitchen counter. After writing something down, he placed the paper in her palm. "I've missed you, Emily, and I hope you'll let me take you out tomorrow. Here's my phone number. Just call me and let me know when you've decided if you'd like to spend some time together."

She mutely nodded, still trying to come to terms with his sudden presence in her home. "Remember that I do love you, Emily. Just give me some time to show you how I feel and how I've changed. I'll try not to disappoint you," he vowed.

Emily nodded, watching him leave, already deciding she would go out with him the following day.

❧

Frank whistled as he prepared for his date with Emily the next day, hoping and praying she would willingly accept him into her life. He had purchased a large heart-shaped box of imported Swiss chocolates and an exquisite diamond pendant.

He ran his fingers over the sparkling gem, imagining the jewel nestled against Emily's caramel-colored throat. He then grabbed his coat, headed out the door, and drove down the familiar route to the Coopers' farm.

Since he was now renting an apartment near Monkton, he arrived at Emily's house in minutes and knocked at her door. He heard the sound of high heels clicking on the kitchen floor before Emily opened the door.

His eyes widened when he saw her wearing a fancy burgundy dress with matching shoes. Her short hair framed her face, drawing attention to her full copper-colored lips and the tiny freckles sprinkled across her nose.

He kissed her hand. "Emily, it's good to see you again."

She nodded, leading him into the living room. "I'm glad to see you, too."

He glanced around the silent house. "Where's your step-mom?" They sat on the tattered couch, and he placed his bag of gifts on the scarred wooden coffee table.

"She's upstairs taking a nap."

"Is she okay?"

"She's fine. After work yesterday and today she was with a family in need with the church outreach. She just came home a few hours ago, so she said she wanted to take a nap." Emily frowned as she glanced up the stairs.

"What's wrong?"

She shrugged. "Laura's been different since her daughter had the baby."

"How?"

She shrugged again. "It's hard to say. I know something has been bothering her for a long time, but she won't talk to me about it."

"Maybe you should ask her about it again. I'm sure if it was something important she would have told you by now."

"No. Don't assume that. Laura can be close-mouthed about a problem for a long time before she says anything about it."

"I'm sure Laura will tell you when she's ready." He paused for a few seconds, glancing around the room. "So, how have you been?"

"Okay, I guess."

"Do Jeremy and Darren still come to help you milk the cows?"

"No, since basketball season started, they said it was too much for them to handle with classes and homework and all. They're both on the basketball team, so that complicates things with their schedules."

"So you're doing the milking by yourself every day?"

"Pretty much. I'll probably get somebody to help me when the weather turns warm again. I think I told you last summer that we go through five hay cuttings, so that's one thing that adds a lot of work during the summer months."

The floral scent of her perfume filled the room with sweetness. He took a deep breath, removing the chocolates and the pendant from the bag. He presented her with his gifts. "I bought these for you. I hope you like them."

She smiled, opening the small box and admiring the diamond pendant. "My goodness! You shouldn't be buying this for me." Her large eyes were full of apprehension as he removed the pendant and placed it on her neck. The gem twinkled against her caramel skin, and Frank was pleased with his purchase. "I also brought you some candy."

"You really shouldn't be buying this for me. I haven't seen you for months and——"

He squeezed her shoulder. "But it looks good on you. If you don't want to wear it, I'll understand." He sighed with relief when she didn't attempt to remove the piece of jewelry. He checked his watch. "We'd better hurry if we want to get there before the comedy show begins."

She fingered the pendant before she stood. "Frank, I need to be honest with you. I still feel funny about your being here so suddenly," she began.

"Emily, I know this is sudden. I probably should have handled this differently and called you first. How about we have a long talk about everything after the show?" When Emily nodded in agreement, they drove to Baltimore to see a Christian comedienne. Frank recalled Emily saying last summer how much she'd wanted to see this entertainer when she came to town, so he was glad he had been able to secure tickets. He tried to enjoy the funny skits during the show, but the sad, despondent look in her eyes haunted him throughout the evening.

Afterward they stopped for hot chocolate at Starbucks. She still seemed sad, so he took her hand, wanting to make her feel better.

She finally smiled, pulling her hand away before sipping her hot drink.

She looked outside at the people passing by the window. "What's on your mind?" he asked.

"I was just thinking that because of you, I'm still living on my farm. Due to the increase of robberies in town, my stepmother insisted we get an alarm system, and we could afford it since you had. . .helped us out financially like that." She squeezed his hand. "Frank, I am truly grateful for what you did for me and Laura. I really am. I promise we'll pay the money back," she said softly, her eyes suddenly filling with tears.

His heart skipped a beat when he moved to her side of the table and sat beside her, pulling her into his arms.

"Emily, I'm not worried about the money. Now, what's the matter?"

He relished the feel of her soft hair in the crook of his neck, her tears splattering against his crisp white shirt. "Oh, it's nothing." Her slim brown body fit into his arms perfectly, and he just wanted to hold her forever.

"Well, something must be wrong if you're crying," he persisted, wondering if he would ever understand why women were so strange.

She sniffed. "My life has just been so crazy since my daddy passed. I had to get used to his death; then you showed up, and then I had to get used to the attraction we shared while I came to grips with the fact that you were an unsaved alcoholic. Then you found that incriminating evidence against my father, and I had to get used to the fact that my father wasn't as perfect as I thought him to be." She swallowed, and he continued to hold her. Her hands were shaking, so he took her hands into his, hoping to calm her down. "Then I wondered if there were other facts about my father that I needed to know about." She gave him a watery smile, and he handed her a tissue. She blew her nose and gazed out the window.

"Go on," he urged.

She sniffed loudly. "Then you helped me save my farm, and then you left." She snapped her fingers to emphasize her point. "Even though you said good-bye, I still wondered if you were coming back. And then, months later, you appear on my doorstep to pick up where we left off like nothing was wrong. Yes, things have been a bit crazy since the beginning of last summer, Frank. I feel like my life has been one big emotional roller coaster."

He released her and faced her directly. Her head was down, so he lifted her chin with his fingers, staring directly into her watery eyes. "I hurt you when I left suddenly?" The realization of what he did hit him like a freight train. She nodded. "I'm so sorry, Emily. I was thinking about turning my life around, getting myself back together in Chicago. Leaving seemed to be the best choice." He blew air through his lips, still gazing at her. "Plus, I knew I was in love with you, and I couldn't stand being around you all the time, seeing you, knowing we couldn't be together because I was an alcoholic. I guess I was too selfish to realize how my actions might hurt you."

He pressed his lips to her forehead. "You know, staying wasn't an option for me. When my dad died, you don't know how close I came to drinking again." He took her hand. "I'm still struggling with my alcoholism, and I wanted to be sure that I'd been sober for a long time before I came back here. I wanted to be here with you. I wanted to see you, but I felt like if I were here and started drinking again, things wouldn't have worked out with us, and I would have hurt you more by being here instead of staying away." He squeezed her fingers. "Please say you'll forgive me. I do love you, and I hope that you'll believe me eventually."

"I understand why you left, but I still have a hard time starting over with you again." She grabbed a napkin and wiped her eyes. "You know, I was wondering why you bought me those gifts."

He frowned. "What do you mean?"

She touched the pendant. "You leave for six months, and then you show up at my house with this necklace, thinking that things are fine between us and we can start dating."

He shrugged again. "So?"

"So, it almost seems like you're trying to bribe me to go out with you. I feel like you want to use your money to buy nice things to fix the situation so that you can get your way."

"What else am I supposed to do?" He threw his hands up in the air, exasperated.

"Frank! This necklace means nothing to me. It's pretty and I love it, but if I could exchange this necklace for some of your time during your six-month absence so that I wouldn't have had to worry about you so much, I'd exchange it in a heartbeat."

He gripped his cup. "Do you mean to tell me that you would exchange the necklace just so you could have had some contact with me when I disappeared for six months?"

She nodded. "If you had just kept me in the loop and talked to me and told me that you might possibly return, my mind would have been more at ease, and I would have felt better." She continued to caress the necklace. "This necklace is just a piece of jewelry, but your honesty is priceless. Do you understand?"

"I think so. I'm sorry. It's just that. . ."

Emily touched his wrist, urging him to continue. "Go on."

"It's just that, growing up, my father wasn't always nice to my mother. He had affairs, and my mother would get upset and cry. He always managed to buy her something—expensive jewelry or a trinket that she would like. Things would be better for a few months before he started acting up again." He sipped his chocolate. "I thought women liked getting nice things, and I thought it showed how much I want to spend time with you."

He looked out the window, staring at the people walking down the sidewalk. "You know how I take a special interest in Trish's children and how I used to mentor boys at the rec center in Chicago?"

"Yes."

"Well, while I was home, I thought about why I'm so passionate about kids having a father in their lives, especially boys. As I've been meeting with alcoholic support groups, talking things out, I've discovered that my passion for that stems from the way I wished my dad had treated me. He always provided for Trish and me financially, but we didn't do a whole lot of things together as a family. He was gone a lot, working long hours, and he was always going away on business trips."

"Frank, you've never told me any of this before."

"Honey, I don't think I even realized half this stuff about myself until recently."

"It sounds like your time away has given you a chance to really think about your life."

He agreed before taking another sip of his hot drink. "Anyway, Julie, when I was married to her, used to complain about my buying her things after we'd had an argument. She said my generosity didn't make the problem go away and that we needed to talk about it."

She nodded. "Julie was right. But you're just following your father's example, so it's understandable why you would think that a new item might make a woman feel better." She changed the subject. "Were you able to straighten out your relationship with your parents?"

"I'm glad I went to Chicago, because both Trish and I were able to spend some quality time with my father before he passed. We convinced him to accept Christ before his death."

Emily squeezed his hand. "That's wonderful, Frank."

He nodded. "Things are still a little shaky with my mom. In my heart, I feel I've forgiven them for the way they treated Julie, but I still feel bad for my mom. She's still not saved, but Trish and I are working on her. She's grieving so hard for my dad, and Trish and I are doing all that we can to console her."

"At least Trish is still there in Chicago with her. Did your mother object to your leaving again?"

Frank thought about his mother. "Yes, she objected a lot, but I felt strongly about coming back and seeing you again, and I didn't think it was right for me to stay away. She accused me of abandoning my familial duties since my dad had passed. I reminded her that Trish and her family were in Chicago to keep her company."

"Does she know about me?"

"Yes."

"Does she know that I'm a dairy farmer? I know she didn't approve of Julie's background. I'm not from a privileged background, either."

He didn't want to tell her that his mother already objected to his dating her. Since he sensed Emily was already apprehensive about having a relationship with him, he certainly didn't want to scare her away with that fact. "Let's not talk about my mom right now. Let's talk about us."

She stared at the whipped cream and marshmallows floating on her cup of hot chocolate. "Frank, I'm not sure this is such a good idea."

His heart skipped a beat. "What do you mean?"

She pointed to the hot chocolate. "Us spending time together, drinking hot chocolate, dating, whatever you call it."

His mouth dropped open, and he touched the tiny mole on the side of her neck. "Emily, I've told you how much I've changed over the last six months. The least you can do is give me a chance to prove myself. Why would you not want us to date?"

She looked at him, her eyes sparkling with fear and apprehension. "I can't deny there is something between us, but even though you're saved now, I find it hard to trust you." She raised her hands in the air. "You've been gone for six months with hardly any contact. If we start dating and then I get emotionally involved with you, what's to stop you from leaving again for another six months?" She fingered the paper mug. "What if you leave again and never come back?"

"Oh, Emily." He tried to pull her into his arms, but she pushed him away. "Frank, you need to give me some time and space to think and pray about this. I feel so confused right now."

He closed his eyes briefly, silently praying for a way to make her understand how much he truly loved her. "I'll be praying for you, too, Emily."

She raised her eyebrows. "You'll be praying for me?"

He nodded. "Yes. I'll be praying that God will make you understand just how much you mean to me. I'll also pray that God will soften your heart to forgive me for leaving you for six months." He stopped and swallowed, still trying to find the right words to say. "I'll also hope and pray that Jesus will allow you to trust me. I know you don't trust me right now, but maybe, just maybe, that'll change."

"It just sounds so odd, you speaking of prayer."

He shrugged. "I told you I've accepted Christ. I'm a saved man, so of course I'm going to pray."

She seemed to be thinking about his statement, weighing his words. "I do need some time to think about this." Her toffee-colored fingers caressed the sparkling diamond nestled on her neck. "I also think you should take your gift back. It's not right for me to accept such an expensive item from you if I'm not sure what's going to happen between us."

"Keep the necklace."

"But, Frank, I really don't feel comfortable accepting things from you."

He sighed. "Why don't you keep the gifts until you decide what you'd like to do? Think and pray about it for as long as you want. Take all the time you need. I understand why you're hesitant about spending time with me again. When you feel more comfortable about it, just let me know, and we can talk about it." They were silent as the whirring sound of the espresso machine filled the shop. Frank finally spoke. "Come on, I'll take you home now."

She nodded, then stood and gathered her coat. "All right." She remained silent as he helped her put on her coat, and they walked to his car.

thirteen

The following Sunday, Emily stood in the pew, accompanying the choir with the rest of the congregation in the closing hymn. Laura grabbed her arm after they exited the sanctuary. Before Laura could speak, Kelly walked toward them from the front of the church, still sporting her red and white choir robe. "Emily, I've been meaning to call you for the last few days, but I've been busy." She seemed slightly out of breath, and tendrils of dark hair fell into her face.

Laura squeezed Emily's arm. "Kelly, did you know Frank was back in town? I just saw him in the sanctuary."

Kelly frowned, staring at the older woman. "Of course I do, Mrs. Cooper! Didn't you know?"

"No, I didn't." She gazed at her stepdaughter. "Now I understand why you've been so quiet and moody the last couple of days. Why didn't you tell me that Frank was back? Have you had a chance to speak with him yet?"

Frank entered the foyer. "Yes, Laura, I've seen your daughter. Twice."

Emily glanced at Frank. "Hi, Frank."

He smiled, touching her shoulder. "Hi, Emily."

Mrs. Cooper spoke to the accountant. "You've changed so much over the last six months, Frank, I barely recognized you sitting in front of the sanctuary. How are you?" She embraced him, and he smiled.

"I've been okay. A lot has been going on in my life since I've been gone."

Laura's brown eyes twinkled. "Well, we're going out to lunch. Why don't you join us and tell us all about it?"

He looked at Emily briefly before focusing on Laura again. "I'm afraid I can't, but you ladies have yourselves a nice lunch." He waved, following the rest of the crowd out of the church.

"Emily Jane Cooper, what in the world is going on here?" Her stepmother folded her arms in front of her chest, impatiently tapping her foot. Kelly stared at Emily also, and Emily felt as if she were being judged by a jury.

"Emily!" Kelly grabbed her arm, and Emily gazed at her best friend.

"What?"

"Let me put my choir robe away. Then we can go to lunch, and you can tell me and your mom what's happening between you and Frank."

"Okay."

"Hi, Emily." Christine approached, wearing a new dress. She held up her purse. "I got a new bag on sale at one of the shops at the Inner Harbor, fifty percent off."

"Why did you buy the purse?" asked Kelly.

Christine pursed her lips. "I had a huge argument with my sister the other day. When I got off the phone, I just wanted something to make myself feel better, so I went shopping. I think I did pretty good since I only purchased two items and one of them was on sale."

Emily's stepmother fingered the purse. "It looks lovely, Christine. We're about to go to lunch if you'd like to join us."

Soon they were seated amid the Sunday afternoon crowd at the Wagon Wheel. Emily told her mother, Kelly, and Christine about the two times she'd seen Frank and about her fears. "I've been praying about it, and I want to date Frank, I really do, but it's just so hard to trust him after all that's happened. Also, I'm wondering what will happen when he has rough times. Will he still turn to alcohol? I know he's saved, but that doesn't mean he's perfect."

"Neither are you," Kelly retorted.

"What's that supposed to mean?" asked Emily.

"Frank explained why he left. He told you himself how messed up his life was before he found Christ. He finally admitted he had a problem with alcohol, he beat his habit, he's accepted Christ, and now he's back. It may have taken him some time to be honest with you, but I can understand why he stayed away."

"But he could have said something before now. He only e-mailed me a couple of times, and that was it."

Laura touched Emily's hand. "Honey, Kelly is right. I'm not saying you need to pick up where you left off, because you're right to be cautious, but maybe you can get to know each other again."

Emily shook her head. "I don't know."

Laura continued to speak. "Emily, I think Frank's silence was just his way of protecting you. He feared he wasn't strong enough to stay away from alcohol. He didn't want you to get emotionally involved with him if he ended up drinking again."

Kelly nodded. "I agree, Mrs. Cooper. I think it's good that you were honest with Frank. He knows he's made a mistake, and I'm sure he feels bad about hurting you. But I also sense that he felt as if he had no choice, because if he was here and he messed up again, he would have ended up hurting you even more."

Christine spoke. "I agree with Mrs. Cooper and Kelly. You need to date Frank and just take it slow. Get to know each other again. He's already told you that he loves you and wants to give you two a chance." She twirled the pearls around her neck. "You know, if you don't at least give him a chance, I think you'll regret it."

She glanced at her friend. "Do you think so?"

Christine nodded firmly. "Yes, I do think so. I could see you wondering for years and years what would have happened if you'd given Franklin Reese a chance way back when."

Emily ate the rest of her meal in silence, allowing Kelly, Christine, and her stepmother to chat without her input. At one point, Laura pulled out her wallet and showed Kelly and Christine recent pictures of her grandbaby.

Emily's mind was still plagued with thoughts about Frank when she milked the cows later that evening.

❧

The following Sunday, Emily entered the sanctuary with her stepmother. She anxiously scanned the crowd of parishioners sitting in the wooden pews.

"Looking for somebody in particular?" Laura whispered in her ear.

Emily gritted her teeth, wishing her affection for Frank wasn't so obvious. She wondered where he was. The service was about to start, and he still had not shown up.

The choir entered the choir loft, and the small church was suddenly filled with holy music.

Kelly joyfully sang the opening hymn with the rest of the choir. Emily attempted to sway to the music, but thoughts of Frank and his whereabouts filled her mind.

When the choir completed their selections, Pastor Brown stepped into the pulpit, and his deep, booming voice filled the sanctuary. "Before I start the sermon this morning, I wanted to introduce one of our new members. I assume a lot of you have met Franklin Reese."

Emily's heart skipped a beat as she clutched her Bible. A few of the parishioners nodded in response.

"Well, he's been through a life-changing experience, and he's requested that I allow him to tell you all about it. So, here's Franklin Reese!" He raised his hand toward the pulpit door, and Frank stepped onto the dais. They shared a handshake before Frank stood in front of the microphone.

Emily openly stared at the man who was slowly capturing

her heart. He looked handsome sporting a dark suit and a cream-colored shirt and tie.

"Good morning."

Parishioners loudly responded to Frank's greeting.

"I've come to tell you this morning about how I came to accept Christ into my life."

During the next fifteen minutes, Emily listened to Frank tell details of his troubled college years and about the first time he realized he was an alcoholic. He then spoke of his sobriety, his first marriage, his strong love for his wife, her salvation, and her sudden violent death. "Friends, when my wife died, I felt a part of me had died also. I was mad, angry, and bitter. I was upset with my parents since they didn't accept my wife because of her background." He told of his return to alcoholism, the joy and warmth he received when attending Monkton Christian Church, and his support from Devon Crandall and the alcoholic support group. He mentioned there was a certain parishioner who urged him to accept Christ, and without mentioning a name, Frank's eyes met Emily's. He told of his salvation at Cylburn Arboretum and his sudden flee back to his hometown, hoping to put his life back in order.

He ended his testimony by telling how Christ had made a difference in his life. "My life is far from perfect, and I still have problems, but they don't seem like such a burden now that I'm relying on Jesus." A tear glistened on Frank's cheek as he spoke of the deep love he had for his Savior. The congregation stood, applauding Frank's courage in openly proclaiming his salvation journey.

Emily barely heard Pastor Brown's message afterward because she was still thinking about Frank's speech.

❧

A few weeks following Frank's testimony, Emily walked toward her house after milking the cows. She removed her barn boots before opening the door and entering her home. The scent of chicken filled the air, and Laura removed a pan of biscuits from the oven. "Hi, Emily."

Emily sniffed. "Hi, Mom. You made chicken and dumplings and biscuits?" Her stomach grumbled with hunger, and she looked forward to the meal.

Laura smiled, but her eyes seemed sad as she looked at Emily. "Yes, I haven't made it in a long time, and I know how much you like my chicken and dumplings." Once Emily had washed up and changed, she joined her stepmother at the table. After Laura said grace, Emily piled her plate with food. "I made chocolate cake for dessert." Emily smiled before she stuffed a bite in her mouth.

Laura tapped her foot, sipping a cup of coffee, and Emily savored the tasty meal. "Aren't you going to eat?"

Laura shook her head. "I'm too nervous to eat."

Emily stopped eating, dropping her fork on her plate. "Why would you be nervous?"

Her stepmother's hand shook as she set her cup back on the saucer. "You've probably guessed that something heavy has been on my mind since Becky had her baby."

"Yes. When Frank came back to town, that was one of the first things I told him. I knew something was bothering you, but I didn't know what it was."

Laura sipped her coffee. "Well, you know how I've always wanted to improve my relationship with my daughters."

Emily nodded.

Laura shrugged. "I missed a lot of their childhoods because my ex-husband was granted custody. Although I saw them for a few weeks each summer, I still felt as if they resented me, especially Becky. She was only five when the divorce happened, and I sometimes think she blames me for what happened to her."

"Children are not always rational."

Laura shrugged. "Adults are not always rational, either." She stared at her coffee cup as she continued to speak. "I think Becky still blames me a little bit for the divorce, but we've been discussing what's happened over the years, and I think we're getting closer. When Becky had her baby and we spent a lot of time together, she told me that she and her husband had discussed it, and eventually she wants to go back to work. She said she was tired of being a housewife and mother full-time and she wanted to reenter the workforce."

"But Becky has three kids now, and all of them are under five. Won't she and her husband be paying a lot in daycare costs if she decides to work again full-time?"

Laura took Emily's hand, looking directly into her eyes. "They won't have to pay as much in daycare costs if I'm taking care of their kids."

Emily's heart skipped a beat, and she gasped. "You're leaving?"

Laura nodded, squeezing Emily's hand. "Honey, I know when I first married your father, you and I got off to a rocky start, but I've grown to love you as a daughter."

"I love you, too, Mom."

"I've told you how I've always regretted not having a better relationship with my daughters. This is something that I really want to do. I can be there to help raise my grandchildren and solidify my relationship with Becky."

Emily wiped the tears from her eyes. "I'm going to be on this farm all by myself." She did not find the thought to be soothing. She recalled how empty the house felt when Laura was gone the other two times.

"Honey, I know. I've been struggling with this decision since I returned last September. That's what's been bothering me so much. I never said anything, because Becky didn't have a job yet."

Emily sniffed as Laura handed her a tissue. As she dried her eyes, she noticed that Laura was crying also. "So Becky's found a job?"

"Yes. She's going to be starting in one month, so I'm not leaving right away, but I promised her I would be there to help out when it's time for her to start her new job. We've already spoken about the finances, and she'll be paying me an amount comparable to what I'd been earning in the lunch room at the school."

The shocking news rocked Emily's world, and the two women embraced before Emily finished her meal.

෴

After Laura made her announcement about leaving, Emily spent the next few weeks thinking about her situation with Frank and praying about it. When Laura did leave, it was heartbreaking for Emily. She drove her stepmother to the airport and promised that if she found adequate help on the farm, she'd come and visit Laura and her family within the next year. She still participated in her church book club, and she was still involved in the singles ministry. She kept a busy routine, trying to figure out what to do about Frank. She didn't mention the matter anymore to Laura, Kelly, or Christine, but left it solely in the Lord's hands.

When Frank had been in town for a month and a half, Emily fell to her knees before bedtime, continuing to seek the Lord's guidance. "Lord," she whispered, "let me know what You want me to do. I keep thinking about Frank. When I see him at church, worshipping and praising You on Sunday, I just want to walk up the aisle, sit beside him, and praise You with him. I want to spend time with him and get to know him all over again now that he's a Christian. Does this mean he's the right man for me, Lord?" When she finished her prayer, calming peace flowed through her.

She slid between her crisp, clean cotton sheets, and when she awakened the next morning, she knew what she had to do.

fourteen

The next day was Saturday, and after Emily milked her cows and did some errands, she showered and changed into her favorite blue jeans and red shirt.

She had already discovered the location of Frank's new apartment from the gossip she'd heard through the church grapevine. She'd also heard that he volunteered every other Saturday at the rec center in a nearby town. She drove to his apartment building in Monkton, saying a silent prayer during the entire journey. She took a deep breath and knocked on his door, wondering if she should have called before traipsing to his apartment unannounced.

The rusty hinges creaked when the door swung open. "Emily!"

Emily clenched her hands together, staring at Frank. "Frank, I wanted to talk with you. I hope it's all right."

He smiled, stroking his beard. "Emily, you're always welcome in my home. Come in." She stepped into the living room, trying to ignore the clothes and newspapers scattered on the hardwood floor. A heavenly scent of tomatoes and spices spilled from the small kitchen. "What are you cooking?"

"Spaghetti and meatballs. I made some garlic bread, too."

Surprised, she glanced into the kitchen before looking at Frank again. A disturbing thought fluttered through her mind. "You made all this for lunch?"

"Yes."

"Are you expecting somebody?" Had she waited too long to give him an answer, and he'd already started dating? She noticed how the single women at church swarmed after Frank like bees to honey.

"No."

"Then why did you make all this for lunch?"

He motioned toward the kitchen, not answering her question. "I'm getting ready to eat right now if you're interested." He caressed her with his dark brown eyes, and her heart thudded. When her tummy rumbled, he chuckled. "You still haven't changed. I see you still have a noisy stomach."

She chuckled, and he led her into the kitchen and pulled out a chair for her. She sat, and he served up plates of spaghetti and meatballs, salad, and garlic bread. "I've missed having home-cooked food since Laura's been gone."

Frank nodded. "I can understand that. Have you heard from her?"

"We call each other regularly. She sounds happy, and I think she's glad that she's growing closer to her daughter and her grandchildren." Frank took her hand and bowed his head. In his deep, strong voice, he thanked the Lord for their food. Emily said amen and squeezed his hand. She took a bite of the food and moaned. "Oh my!"

"What's the matter?"

She licked her lips, taking another bite of spaghetti before sampling the crunchy garlic bread. "This is the best spaghetti I've ever had." She sampled more food. "Mmm. This garlic bread is excellent!"

He laughed, watching her eat. "I'm glad you like it so much."

"I can't believe you made all this yourself."

"I don't use spaghetti sauce out of a jar. I make my own, and I made the garlic bread myself, too."

"You cook?" She looked at him, and she felt as if she was seeing a new Frank, a different Frank from the way he was eight months ago.

"Yes, I cook."

"But when I went to your old apartment, you had pizza boxes and empty take-out containers all over the room. I thought you didn't know how to cook."

They ate in silence, enjoying their meal. When they were finished, they took their lemonade into the living room, and Frank invited her to sit. "I'm glad you came by. I wanted to talk to you about something."

She sat on the expensive leather couch. "Good, I wanted to talk to you, too."

"You were asking about my cooking earlier?"

"Yes."

"Well, cooking is something I used to do all the time before Julie died. When she died, I started drinking, and I just stopped doing the things I loved, like cooking and working out." He sipped his lemonade. "I was so bitter and angry that the only thing that brought me pleasure was alcohol. You know when I left you for six months and my dad died?"

She nodded, encouraging him to continue.

"Well, I was a real mess back then."

"I know, you told me that."

"No, I didn't tell you how bad of a mess I was. When my dad died, I was so afraid that I was going to start drinking again that I took a month-long leave of absence from work. Even though I was saved, the urge to drink consumed me so much that I went to a medical doctor, and he had to give me medicine to help with my cravings."

She touched his arm. "Are you still on the medicine?"

"No, I stopped taking it a few months before I decided to come back here. But I was off work for a whole month, helping my mother out and just straightening out my life. There's an alcoholic support group that meets each day in Chicago. It's not always the same people, but I made sure I was there every day. Being with the other members helped me stay sober. I read my Bible like crazy. I was drinking in the Word, and I had so many questions about the scriptures. My church in Chicago was awesome, and they answered all my questions about God and the Bible. I found that I had a lot of learning to do." He pointed toward his Bible. "I don't think I could've made it through this whole ordeal if it weren't for God."

He paused for a moment, then said softly, "You know, Emily, I love reading the scriptures. There's so much wisdom between those pages." He looked toward the window for a minute, as if thinking of what he should say. "Anyway, during my absence, I learned that I not only had to continue placing my faith in God, but I also had to get into the things that brought me pleasure."

"Like cooking?"

He squeezed her hand. "Yes, like cooking. It's something to do to keep my mind off drinking."

"Do you still have the urge to drink?"

He looked at her. "Honey, the urge to drink never goes away; you just have to learn to be strong and not act on it. It's scary thinking about not ever having another drink, but you have to take it one day at a time."

She blew air through her lips. "I didn't realize that."

"I had to let you know all this. I'd still like us to get to know each other again. I'm different now."

"That's what I wanted to talk to you about."

"Oh?"

"Yes. I think I'd like to give us a chance. I wondered if we could get to know each other as friends again."

His lips touched her nose. "I'm too attracted to you to be just your friend, but I'd like to spend time with you again."

She smiled at him. "I'm attracted to you, too. And I have an admission of my own to make."

He chuckled. "What's that?"

"I'm a lousy cook."

He laughed. "I know. You told me that when I first met you. Maybe my cooking skills will balance everything out between us."

She smiled. "Yes, maybe your cooking skills will balance everything out."

&

During the next few months, Frank continued to struggle with his decision to ask Emily to marry him. Even though they were getting to know each other better, he still faltered as far as his alcoholism was concerned. It was a daily struggle, and he prayed each day for the strength to let go and trust himself and believe in the Lord enough to trust his decision to marry Emily.

As he got to know Emily again, he found his love for her grew as the days passed. Since Laura was gone, Emily was out at the farm alone, and he often worried about her living by herself in the country, running the farm solo. He visited often after work, and he realized she wasn't kidding when she said she couldn't cook. His frequent late-evening visits often included takeout. Sometimes in the evenings, while she was in the barn milking the cows, he'd stop at the grocery store to buy food to make dinner for her.

He knew he had really fallen hard for her when he arrived unexpectedly at five in the morning on a Saturday. He'd worn his oldest clothing and a pair of battered sneakers. After parking in the driveway, he traipsed to the familiar barn. The cows were chained in their stalls, eating their piles of food. He recalled Emily telling him about the corn, soybeans, and alfalfa they grew to make feed for the cows. A clear liquid squished through the pipes, and Frank found Emily in the room where the milk tank and sink were located. "Frank!" Her eyes shone with delight as they embraced. "What are you doing here?"

"I know you like having somebody to help you milk the cows, so I came to give you a hand." Since Emily had been milking the cows most of her life, he figured he'd be more of a hindrance than a help. But he was determined to learn how to milk so he could help her eventually. He gestured toward the sink. "What are you doing?"

She explained that she was cleaning the pipes and the equipment with an acid and water solution before she started milking. He washed his hands before he followed her as she went into the barn carrying the mobile milking units. She gave him a pair of gloves, patiently explaining how she cleaned the udders of each cow using an iodine dipper. She left and returned with a steaming bucket of liquid. "I could have carried that in here for you," he said.

She smiled, patiently explaining he could carry it next time if he came back to milk again. Since he felt so uneasy cleaning the teats and udders of each cow and attaching the units, Emily ended up doing most of the milking herself. Nevertheless, it felt good to be out in the barn with her, watching her do the chores. He found that he was a better help once the cows were milked. She pushed a cart full of feed and handed him a shovel. "After milking we feed the cows grain, soybeans, and corn feed." She told him what to do. "Just shovel some in front of each stall. After they're done, we need to let them out to graze a bit. I'm going to clean the milking equipment." As he shoveled feed, he glanced at the pipes, noting that clear liquid again swished through them as Emily did her cleanup. Once they'd cleaned the floor and let the cows out, he followed her to the porch. She removed her barn boots, and he took off his shoes, wiggling his toes.

"Thanks for helping me this morning, Frank."

He shrugged. "I'm not sure if I was much help."

She touched his arm. "You were a big help." When they'd washed up, Frank made bacon, eggs, and toast for breakfast. Once he said grace over their meal and they were eating, Emily told him something. "My sister, Sarah, called me last night."

"Did she want money?"

"Yes."

"How much did she want?"

"She said she needed two hundred dollars to pay her phone bill. If she doesn't pay it soon, they're going to turn her phone off."

"Are you going to give it to her?"

Emily shrugged. "I don't know. I told her I'd have to think and pray about it. I said I'd call her back in a couple of days to let her know what I'd decided to do." She sipped her juice. "Have you spoken to your mother lately?"

He sighed, spreading butter and jelly on his toast. "Yes."

"How is she doing?"

"She's doing okay." He didn't bother to mention that his mother had not been vocal about his dating life in a long time. He still wasn't sure if she was learning to accept his choices or if she had more pressing things on her mind. "Trish spends time with her every week, so I'm glad about that."

"How are the kids doing?"

"They're doing fine. Next month is Regina's birthday. I'm flying up to Chicago for that." He stopped eating and took her hand. "I'd like for you to come with me if you can get somebody to do the milking for you."

"I'd love to come with you, Frank, but I can't make any promises. I'll see if I can find somebody to do the chores for me the weekend of the party."

They continued to eat in silence for a few minutes before he mentioned he was going to the rec center later on. "You know, I didn't realize how much I missed spending time with young people until I started doing it again."

"Yeah, I can tell you enjoy it. It's nice of you to spend time mentoring the kids at the center." After a few moments, she touched his arm. "I enjoyed having you with me this morning to milk the cows. It was nice."

He took her hand, squeezing her fingers. "I enjoyed doing it with you. Is it okay if I come and help you milk on the weekends?"

Emily returned his squeeze. "Yes, I'd like that very much."

Later that day, Frank found a store in Monkton that sold barn boots. When he returned to Emily's for the next milking, he brought his new footwear with him. He left his new barn boots at Emily's, placing them right beside hers.

≈

When Frank had been helping Emily milk cows for a couple of months, he finally felt it was time to ask her to marry him. On the day he purchased the ring from the jeweler, he called his mother. "Hello, Franklin." His mother was one of the few relatives who still called him by his full name.

He hesitated. "Mom, hi."

"You've got a worried tone in your voice, son."

"How are you?"

His mother spoke for five minutes about her health and how her regular visits with Trish and her grandchildren were going. Frank blurted his news before he lost his courage. "I'm going to ask Emily to marry me."

"Emily? That farmer you told me about when you came home?"

"Yes, Mom. You can't treat her the way you treated Julie. I don't like that kind of behavior." He failed to mention that his parents' actions had intensified his grief after Julie's violent death. "I love her too much to hurt her like that. She's a strong, proud woman, and she's running that farm by herself right now." When she remained silent, he mentally said a quick prayer before he reminded her how he'd met Emily through his job and how they'd grown closer in recent months. "If she says yes, then she'll be a part of the family."

"This is so sudden," she began.

Frank still wondered what was going through his mother's brain. "It's not so sudden. I just explained how long I've known her. I love her, Mom, and it'll hurt me if you reject her for superficial reasons." When his mother remained silent, he finally ended the call. Once he'd hung up the phone, he fell to his knees. "Lord, please, if this is your will and Emily says yes, please make everything work out with my mom. Amen."

≈

When Emily arrived at Frank's apartment for their Saturday night dinner date, the sight of the lit tapered candles on the table made her stop and stare. "Why are we eating by candlelight?" She had been a bit suspicious when he'd called earlier, saying he would not be by that evening to help her with the milking.

He pulled her into his arms, kissing her nose. "I just wanted to share a romantic dinner with you. What's wrong with that?"

She shook her head. "Nothing."

"I think you sometimes forget how much I enjoy your company." He led her to the table. "Let's eat."

When he placed the shrimp cocktail on the table, she looked at him. "Shrimp cocktail?"

He took her hand, asking the Lord to bless their food. Once they said their amens, he commented, "I made crab cakes and rice pilaf for dinner."

"All my favorites." When he continued to hold her hand, she wondered when they were going to dig into their meal. He kissed her fingers, and she closed her eyes, enjoying the feel of his lips against her skin.

"I have a question for you." His voice was low and husky, and his dark eyes shone in the candlelight.

He released her hand and pulled a small velvet box out of his pocket. He presented it to her. When she popped the box open, the diamond solitaire ring glittered. "Frank!"

"Will you marry me, Emily? You know how much I love you."

"Yes, I'll marry you. I love you, Frank!"

He pulled her into his arms, and they shared a blissful kiss.

epilogue

Frank stood at the altar of Monkton Christian Church, his smile so wide he thought his face would split apart. Christine, Kelly, Trish, and Emily's sister, Sarah, served in the wedding as bridesmaids. Their canary yellow dresses looked becoming as the bright sunlight streamed through the church's stained glass windows. Mark, decked out in his tuxedo, was a junior groomsman, and Regina served as a junior bridesmaid.

His mother sat in the front of the church, looking uncomfortable as she scanned the crowd. Both he and Trish were trying to convince their mother that her strict way of judging others was wrong, and so far she'd been cordial to Emily, not shunning her the way she'd shunned Julie.

Laura Cooper sat in the front row, crying openly. Since Frank was going to live with Emily on her dairy farm, Laura had confided to him that she felt better about her decision to leave and move in with her daughter.

Frank's heart palpitated when Emily walked down the aisle. Her white silky dress complemented her smooth brown skin. As Devon Crandall and his other friends from church served as ushers, Frank and Emily vowed to love each other forever.

A Letter To Our Readers

Dear Reader:
In order that we might better contribute to your reading enjoyment, we would appreciate your taking a few minutes to respond to the following questions. We welcome your comments and read each form and letter we receive. When completed, please return to the following:

Fiction Editor
Heartsong Presents
PO Box 719
Uhrichsville, Ohio 44683

1. Did you enjoy reading *Milk Money* by Cecelia Dowdy?
   ❑ Very much! I would like to see more books by this author!
   ❑ Moderately. I would have enjoyed it more if

   _____

   _____

   _____

2. Are you a member of **Heartsong Presents**? ❑ Yes ❑ No
   If no, where did you purchase this book? _____

   _____

3. How would you rate, on a scale from 1 (poor) to 5 (superior), the cover design? _____

4. On a scale from 1 (poor) to 10 (superior), please rate the following elements.

   ____ Heroine   ____ Plot
   ____ Hero   ____ Inspirational theme
   ____ Setting   ____ Secondary characters

5. These characters were special because? _____

_____

_____

6. How has this book inspired your life? _____

_____

_____

7. What settings would you like to see covered in future
   Heartsong Presents books? _____

_____

_____

8. What are some inspirational themes you would like to see
   treated in future books? _____

_____

_____

9. Would you be interested in reading other **Heartsong
   Presents** titles? ☐ Yes ☐ No

10. Please check your age range:

    ☐ Under 18   ☐ 18-24

    ☐ 25-34   ☐ 35-45

    ☐ 46-55   ☐ Over 55

Name _____

Occupation _____

Address _____

City, State, Zip _____

Presents

Great Inspirational Romance at a Great Price!

Heartsong Presents books are inspirational romances in
contemporary and historical settings, designed to give you an
enjoyable, spirit-lifting reading experience. You can choose
wonderfully written titles from some of today's best authors like
Wanda E. Brunstetter, Mary Connealy, Susan Page Davis,
Cathy Marie Hake, Joyce Livingston, and many others.

When ordering quantities less than twelve, above titles are $2.97 each.
Not all titles may be available at time of order.